embrace
me

J. KENNER
NEW YORK TIMES BESTSELLING AUTHOR

Also by J. Kenner

His touch is her sin. Her love is his salvation

My Fallen Saint

My Beautiful Sin

My Cruel Salvation

Stark Security

Charismatic. Dangerous. Sexy as hell.

Shattered With You

Shadows Of You

(prequel to Broken With You)

Broken With You

Ruined With You

Wrecked With You

Destroyed With You

Memories of You (novella)

Ravaged With You

The Steele Books/Stark International:

He was the only man who made her feel alive.

Say My Name

On My Knees

Under My Skin

Take My Dare (includes short story Steal My Heart)

Stark International Novellas:

Meet Jamie & Ryan–so hot it sizzles.

Tame Me

Tempt Me

Tease Me

S.I.N. Trilogy:

It was wrong for them to be together…

…but harder to stay apart.

Dirtiest Secret

Hottest Mess

Sweetest Taboo

Most Wanted:

Three powerful, dangerous men.

Three sensual, seductive women.

Wanted

Heated

Ignited

Stark World Stories:

Set in the Stark universe.

Wicked Grind

Wicked Dirty

Wicked Torture

Justify Me

Man of the Month

Who's your man of the month …?

Down On Me

Hold On Tight

Need You Now

Start Me Up

Get It On

In Your Eyes

Turn Me On

Shake It Up

All Night Long

In Too Deep

Light My Fire

Walk The Line

Royal Cocktail (bonus book)

*Bar Bites: A Man of the Month Cookbook

(by J. Kenner & Suzanne M. Johnson)

Blackwell-Lyon:

Heat, humor & a hint of danger

Lovely Little Liar

Pretty Little Player

Sexy Little Sinner

Tempting Little Tease

Lost in Shadows

Surrender to Dawn

Extraordinarily Yours

Writing as Julie Kenner

Sexy paranormal rom-com romps!

So (Very!) Much More than the Girl Next Door

Mayhem, Matchmakers, and a Bit of Bewitching

The Charmed Affair of an Invisible Bodyguard

The "Super" Secret Life of an Accidental Daddy

Never Trust a Rogue on a Magical Mission

How a Sexy Hero and a Marvelous Makeover (Sorta!) Saved the World

The Seductive Charm of a Sexy Shifter

Other Paranormal Reads

Short and Sexy

His Wicked Touch

Seducing Sin

Tempting Fate

Visit www.jkenner.com for a complete booklist

Praise for J. Kenner's Novels

"PERFECT for fans of *Fifty Shades of Grey* and *Bared to You*. *Release Me* is a powerful and erotic romance novel that is sure to make adult romance readers sweat, sigh and swoon." *Reading, Eating & Dreaming Blog*

"I will admit, I am in the 'I loved *Fifty Shades*' camp, but after reading *Release Me*, Mr. Grey only scratches the surface compared to Damien Stark." *Cocktails and Books Blog*

"It is not often when a book is so amazingly well-written that I find it hard to even begin to accurately describe it . . . I recommend this book to everyone who is interested in a passionate love story." *Romancebookworm's Reviews*

"The story is one that will rank up with the *Fifty Shades* and Cross Fire trilogies." *Incubus Publishing Blog*

"The plot is complex, the characters engaging, and J. Kenner's passionate writing brings it all perfectly together." *Harlequin Junkie*

A sizzling, intoxicating, sexy read!!!! J. Kenner had me devouring Wicked Dirty, the second installment of *Stark World Series* in one sitting. I loved everything about this book from the opening pages to the raw and vulnerable characters. With her sophisticated prose, Kenner created a love story that had the perfect blend of lust, passion, sexual tension, raw emotions and love. - Michelle, Four Chicks Flipping Pages

embrace me

J. KENNER

NEW YORK TIMES BESTSELLING AUTHOR

M&O

Embrace Me Copyright © 2021 by Julie Kenner
Excerpt from *My Fallen Saint* Copyright © 2020 by Julie Kenner

Cover design by Michele Catalano, Catalano Creative
Cover images by MOELLERTHOMSEN (deposit photos)

ISBN-D: 978-1-953572-22-6
ISBN-P: 978-1-953572-23-3

Published by Martini & Olive Books
V-2021-3-25P-ING

A note from JK

Hello, awesome reader!

As a bonus, I've included four chapters from *My Fallen Saint,* book one of my most recent trilogy. So be sure to keep reading after you finish *Embrace Me*! If you love Damien, you're going to love Devlin Saint, too!

J. Kenn
xxoo

Chapter One

I stand on the bedroom balcony, the doors open behind me as I look out at the morning light glinting on the Pacific. I'm barefoot and fresh from the shower, now wrapped in the extra-large spa-style robe that Damien bought for me when I was pregnant with Anne.

I kept it after she was born even though it swallowed me up because it was so snuggly and comfy. I never expected to actually need it again, but as I press my hand over my very extended belly, I sigh with happiness. Because I *do* need it again. And this time for a boy. B.B.S. we're calling him for now, since we still haven't decided on a name.

Hopefully that will change soon, I think as I rub my hand over my belly. "Because Baby Boy Stark just isn't the kind of name a young man takes with him to college, is it, precious?"

"That's my wife," Damien says, coming up silently and rubbing my neck as I moan with pleasure. "Always bowing to tradition and expectations."

I laugh. "Good morning, Mr. Stark."

"Ms. Fairchild," he says, my name now a term of endearment. Personally, I've gone by Stark since our marriage, but my business was started as Fairchild Development—now Fairchild

& Partners—and I've kept the name simply because I want to grow the business on my own and not because I'm married to a master of the universe.

"And good morning to you, too, B.B.S.," that master of the universe says, abandoning my neck to reach around and cup my baby bump, which is really more of a baby mound these days.

I turn in his arms, sacrificing the gorgeous view of the ocean for the gorgeous view of my husband. He's looking down at me with those incredible dual-colored eyes, his amber eye alight with love, the onyx one dark with strength.

He hasn't shaved yet, and I reach up to brush his cheek, enjoying the feel of his scruff against my palm. His hair is mussed from sleep, as jet black as it was the day we met except for his temples. There's a hint of silver now, something that I think makes him look all the more powerful and sexy, but which I also know is the reflection of more than just the passing years. It's a manifestation of his own scars. The trauma of his past, and the trials of his present. Anne's kidnapping. The death and betrayal of one of his closest friends. Me in danger.

Damien's always stood as a fortress against the horrors of the world, protecting the people he loves, me and the children most of all. But it's not an easy battle, and I know better than anyone how much it has cost him.

He brushes a finger lightly over the tip of my nose. "You're thinking very loudly."

"Am I?" I raise my brows. "Then tell me what I'm thinking."

"That you love me. And," he adds with a smile, "what a coincidence. I'm thinking how much I love you, too."

"It's as if you know me," I trill, moving even closer so he can envelop me in a hug, at least as much as our unborn son's girth allows. "And I was thinking all that and more," I admit. "Mostly, I was thinking about what a great dad you are."

"I can't wait to meet this little guy."

I take a step back, grimacing as B.B.S. shifts position, a foot getting me right in the bladder. "You and me both. But maybe it's good that we still have over two weeks. I think it'll take us that long to decide on a name."

I'd suggested Ash, in honor of my sister, but as much as I love and miss Ashley, it doesn't feel quite right. My best friend, Jamie, had suggested Damien, Jr., but as far as I'm concerned there will only ever be one Damien Stark, and I vetoed that idea.

We've poked around on baby naming sites, but so far, no name has clicked the way Lara and Anne, our daughters' names did. Those, we simply *knew*.

"We'll find his name," Damien says. "I promise you he won't graduate college as Baby Boy Stark."

"It would make for interesting press," I say, making Damien laugh. I force a smile, too, but the reality that the press will inevitably surround our kids is something I do think about, and often. Because no matter what, our children will always be in the spotlight. And as we're about to bring a third child into our family, I have to hope that we'll be good enough parents to help them grow up knowing how to deal with that.

I'm about to share my thoughts with Damien, but the patter of little feet and the cry of "Mommy! Daddy! Mr. G made chocolate pancakes!"

It's Lara, our newly-turned six-year-old. Her four-year-old sister Anne is hurrying behind, shouting, "Choca-pipcakes, Lara! They called choca-pipcakes!"

Lara sighs as she looks at Damien and me, then shakes her head and rolls her eyes, making her long dark hair sway. "Kids," she says, and I almost lose it right then, especially when I feel Damien's body vibrate with laughter.

"Go get started," I manage to tell the girls. "We'll be right there."

They scurry off, and I clap a hand over my mouth as Damien says, "I can't tell you how much I wish I'd recorded that."

"I know. Oh, man." I smile up at him. "They are growing up way too fast."

"They are," he says. "But isn't it a hell of an adventure?

≈

"Mr. G! More juice, pleeeeeeze." Anne's voice echoes through the third-floor kitchen area. This house was unfinished when I first saw it, but this kitchen was already functional. Originally designed for caterers to use during parties, it's cozy and comfortable and has come to completely overshadow the full-blown, restaurant-style commercial kitchen downstairs.

In other words, it's now the heart of our home.

Gregory, who's just settled at the table, starts to rise again. I don't actually know how old Gregory is, but I'm guessing he's at least fifteen years older than Damien. He'd been hired as a valet, a job that expanded into house manager. And after that, he took on the role of nanny when Bree Bernstein, our first nanny, quit to go back to school in New York.

"No, no," I say, waving Gregory down. "I'll get it." I've already finished my avocado and cheese omelet, and I stand carefully and then waddle—yes, *waddle*—to the refrigerator. Right now, it's just me and Gregory and the girls. Damien had coffee earlier, but declined the pancakes or an omelet when Troy Reed, his newest assistant, had called with the first crisis of the day.

"Okay, be good for Mr. G today," I say, as I pour juice, then kiss both girls' foreheads. "Mommy's going to go get dressed. You two do the same, okay? Like big girls."

Lara salutes. "Aye-aye, Captain."

"Aye-aye!" Anne mimics.

I salute back, then share a smile with Gregory before I head out. There's no doubt that he adores our children, but I can't help but think the job is too much for him, what with running the house, too.

"Do you really think Gregory is up for three kids?" I ask Damien, when I find him in the bedroom, finally untethered from his phone. "Especially since this one is going to be a handful." Considering he's just delivered an NFL-worthy kick, that's an assessment about which I'm very confident.

"I've talked to him about it," Damien says. "He swears he loves taking care of them."

"I don't doubt it," I say. "I mean, it's obvious how much he adores the girls, but they exhaust *us*. And Gregory's not as young as he used to be."

"I know. He was looking a little frazzled earlier. And he stopped by the court on his walk over this morning. I noticed he was a little breathless."

A former professional tennis player, Damien habitually works out in the mornings. Sometimes he goes down to our gym, but most days I know I can find him on the court with a ball machine. As for Gregory, Damien built him a small house on the property, just beyond a rise. Close enough to walk, but not so close that we're on top of each other.

"He loves the girls," Damien adds. "I'd hate to have him feel as if he's not part of the family."

"What about part-time?" I suggest, following him into our walk-in closet. So large that it could hold a small motel room, the closet took my breath away the first time I saw it. Honestly, it still does. "Maybe we should look for someone to work part-time? We can tell Gregory it's because we know he has so much to deal with otherwise."

"Maybe," Damien says. "Let's think on it."

"Sure. We don't have to decide right now." I sit on the padded bench and reach around to rub my lower back as I watch Damien finish dressing. He's in a crisp white shirt and the slacks from his suit. I lean back, enjoying the show as he expertly knots a deep red tie, then fastens his cuffs with pewter cufflinks, each accented by a matching red stone. He's already in his shoes, polished to perfection, and now he slips on the dark pewter suit jacket, then runs a hand over his hair before turning to me, one eyebrow raised as if to say, *Well?*

I laugh. "Like you have to ask. You look amazing, and you know it." I stand, grimacing as I do, and move to him, smoothing the material of his shirt just for the pleasure of feeling the silk blend beneath my hand. "A presentation?"

"Potential investor," he says. "A project in Tokyo."

"Right," I say, as if I have a clue what he's talking about. "Well, you'll knock 'em dead."

He always does, after all.

He finishes adjusting his tie, then frowns at me. "Your back?"

"I'll be fine. And it'll be better in couple of weeks for sure."

He comes closer, then pats the opposite end of the bench I'd been sitting on. "Sit here," he says. "Legs on either side."

I do as he says, basically straddling the end as he slides onto the bench behind me, one hand on my shoulder, and the other pressing against my lower back.

"Oh, God, Damien," I say, as his fingers knead the sore muscles. "That feels incredible. Normally, I'd say that nothing beats sex with you, but this is coming very, very close."

He chuckles, then uses the hand from my shoulder to sweep my hair away from my ear as he whispers, "I'm always up for a challenge."

I sigh with pleasure as he runs his fingers through my hair. It's long now, the waves hitting just above my shoulder blade. The perfect length as far as I'm concerned because I can pull it back from my face with a band or a clip if I'm dealing with work or a kid. At times like this, though, I can't deny there are other benefits, too, like the sensual way that it rubs my skin now that Damien is peeling me out of my robe.

My eyes flutter open with the realization that he's undressing me. "Damien," I protest, as the robe drops away.

"Problem?"

I start to protest that, yes, there is definitely a problem. I'm positively huge, and not exactly feeling sexy in my maternity bra and panties. But then he returns one hand to my lower back, the pressure more intense. At the same time, his other hand snakes around my body and eases between my legs. I draw in a breath and decide that my current wardrobe will do just fine.

"Close your eyes, baby," he says as his fingers tease my clit over the cotton panties and he works magic on my back.

"Damien," I murmur, but this time it's not a protest. I have never not been aroused by Damien's touch, but the pregnancy has my hormones on overdrive and one look from him can practically send me spiraling off into an orgasm.

But it's *so* much better if there's a touch to go with the look, and I let myself fall back against him, my eyes closed as he takes control of my body, my senses. As he harnesses that pressure he's building inside me. That craving for release, for an explosion.

"That's right, baby," he murmurs. "Just let me take you there."

I reach up and cup my breasts, spreading my legs wider as I do, and I'm rewarded by Damien's low growl.

"Christ, Nikki, do you know what you do to me? Do you have any idea how much I love you?"

"At least as much as I love you," I whisper, the words forced out ahead of a low gasp and then a cry of pure pleasure as I draw my legs together to stop the sweet torment, trapping Damien's hand between my thighs. "Yes," I gasp, my breath shallow. "Oh, God, yes."

For a moment, he just holds me, both of us breathing hard. Then I force my eyes open and tilt my head back and around so I can see his face. "You're a keeper, Mr. Stark."

He brushes a kiss over my lips. "I'm very glad to hear it."

He eases off the bench, then helps me back into the robe before holding a hand out to ease me to my feet. "And now I have to run."

My eyes dip to his erection, and he flashes a sideways grin. "I need to think about spreadsheets anyway."

I laugh, and he pulls me close for a deeper kiss. "I'll see you tonight."

"Have fun buying the universe, Mr. Stark."

"I always do," he says, and I stand still for a moment, enjoying the view of his ass disappearing into the bedroom.

I start to sit, then realize that I'm buzzing. Or, rather, that the phone I'd dropped into the robe's pocket is buzzing. I know it's not from Damien, and I almost ignore it. But it could be from my partner, Abby, and so I fish it out and glance at the screen.

Immediately, I wish I hadn't.

Because the caller ID on my phone shows the caller as Elizabeth Fairchild.

My mother.

I frown as I decline the call. I haven't spoken to that woman in years. But apparently she still has a knack for destroying an otherwise excellent mood.

Chapter Two

"I'm drowning in resumes," Eric says, then makes a show of banging his blond head on a stack of printouts representing the fifty candidates we've moved into the second round.

Eric and I have spent the last forty minutes discussing the various potentials, and I laugh at his show of frustration because the truth is we still have a long way to go.

He lifts his head and grins at me. "Onward?"

"Onward," I say. "But with coffee. Loaded for you. Decaf for me. See? You should consider yourself lucky."

I start to push back from the table to go get fresh cups for both of us, but he waves me down. "I'll do that," he says, then smirks. "I can get there and back in the time it takes you to get out of that chair."

"You are not nearly as funny as you think you are," I chide, tossing a balled up sheet of paper at him.

He dances out of the way with a grin. "Um, yes I am," he says, then slips into the hallway, taking the last word with him.

I shake my head, amused, as I continue skimming the resumes in my own stack. Eric is not only my newest hire, he was also one of my first. He and my partner, Abby, had joined

Fairchild Development not long after I started it. I'd been overwhelmed with the amount of work I'd taken on—a good thing in terms of building my business, but a bad thing if I wasn't able to make my deadlines.

I ended up hiring help earlier than I'd intended to, and Abby and Eric were the happy result, and the three of us got along great. Abby has since become my partner, but Eric had his mind set on bigger things. He quit to go to New York, something that had saddened me, not only because he really is great at what he does, but because I genuinely enjoy his company.

Not that long ago, though, he'd come back. In New York, he'd been a little fish in a very big pond, whereas with me, he gets to be very hands-on with both coding and clients.

He'd been afraid that I wouldn't want him back, but I can hardly blame someone for their ambition, and I'm thrilled to have him back on the team. I'd been a little worried that he'd be frustrated by Abby's rise in the company, but he's not.

All in all, he's about as perfect as an employee can be, and I think going away made him realize what a good thing he has here. Over the last few months, he's become as much of a right hand as Abby.

And I'm especially grateful for him now that I'm trying to get every single duck in order before I go on maternity leave.

Today's task is to choose five potential interns to bring in for an interview. I add two more to the *No Thank You* pile, then move a USC sophomore's resume to the *Maybe* pile before leaning back in my chair.

"Problem?" Eric asks as he steps back into the conference room. He puts my cup of decaf in front of me, then heads to his side of the table.

"Just wondering if you're sure you want to bring on an intern right now." The idea had been Eric's, something he'd run by Abby and me about two weeks ago. "The timing's not ideal," I add.

He drags his fingers through his hair. "Not perfect," he agrees. "But there's still time."

I glance down at B.B.S., who will be ready to greet the world before I know it. "You've got a few weeks, sure. But we aren't going to hire someone today, and you're going to have to train them before you can use them." I shrug. "Honestly, it might be easier for you and Abby to just divide the work. And if you really get into a bind, you know you can always call me."

He cocks his head and looks me in the eye, then glances down to my baby bump. "I appreciate the offer, but honestly, Nik…?" He grins. "One, I'm thinking you won't want to be disturbed. And two, I'm thinking you're going to be so frazzled, you wouldn't even know what the answer is."

I laugh. He's probably not wrong.

"Besides, if we can get someone in to interview in the next day or so, I'll have almost a week of training before you even leave, right?"

"That's true," I say, picturing the calendar in my head. "This little guy's due in just over three weeks, so I plan to work about ten more days here and then stay home. But until the baby's born, I'll be working. You can call me at home. Or come by. I'll set up the bungalow as an office again, so I'll be there when you need me until I come back here after my leave."

"We'll be fine. You have two little girls who are going to want your time before their brother comes, and then you're going to have a little boy who's going to be very demanding." He grins and indicates himself with a flip of his fingers. "Trust me. I know how much trouble guys can be."

"Fair enough." I look at my stack of potentials, then slide it toward him. "In that case, knock yourself out. I trust you to hire someone perfect."

His eyes widen a little. "What? You're saying you don't want a say?"

"You're going to be the one working the closest with our intern. I think you should do the initial calls and interviews, then get Abby to approve your choice. I'll help if you need me to, but otherwise go for it."

He leans back in his chair, looking only slightly discombobulated. Then he nods. "Yeah. I know what we need. Of course I can do this."

I laugh. "Yes. You can."

"I'll arrange the interviews for when Abby's back," he says referring to my partner who's currently in Dallas meeting with one of our anchor clients. "It'll be easier if she's in the office when I do the interviews. That way I can steer whoever I like over to her office for a second interview."

"See? You're already on top of it." I glance at my notes to see what else we have to cover. "What about Every Note?"

"All good," he says. "I'm heading over to Stark Tower later today to do some training on the new features, but I don't foresee any issues."

"Good." Every Note is a cross-platform, collaborative note-taking app that I designed about the time that I met Damien. It hadn't been finished yet, but I told him about it, and he'd seen the potential. He'd actually wanted to license it right away, but I insisted on starting my business without a connection to my then-boyfriend. Once established, though, I was more than happy to add Stark International to the client list.

I glance at my notepad again and go over a few lingering details until Eric leans back in his chair and groans. "Nikki, you're having a baby, not transferring to the moon. We don't have to go over everything today."

I sigh. He's right of course. I'm in that state where I want to get everything in order before the baby comes. Some books call it nesting. I call it being organized.

"You're right." I narrow my eyes. "But I'm still going to type all this up and send it to you."

He laughs. "You wouldn't be you if you didn't."

I push back and stand, groaning as I get my balance. "All

right, I'm heading out. I have a lunch date, and then I'm going to head home to get ready for tonight. Are you coming?"

"Are you kidding? Of course."

"Good," I say, because even though giving speeches makes me nervous, it's for a good cause and I want my team there, too.

"Business lunch or pleasure?" he asks. "Not that it's any of my business."

"I'm meeting Jamie and Evelyn," I say. "So very much pleasure."

He tells me to say hi to them both, and I promise I will. Then I gather my things and take a ride share to The Patio, a new restaurant in Santa Monica on the Pacific Coast Highway near the Pier. I'd come to work in the Town Car, with Edward —Damien's favorite driver—chauffeuring me, and during this ride, I shoot him a text to let him know I'll need to be picked up at the restaurant in an hour or two.

Soon, I'm settled at a table with my best friend, Jamie Archer Hunter, and Evelyn Dodge, who was one of the first people I met when I moved to Los Angeles. Bold and brassy, Evelyn can always be counted on to say her mind and not pull her punches. And I absolutely love her for that.

Over the years, she's become almost a surrogate mother. A welcome thing, considering the woman whose call I declined this morning never excelled in that role.

"It is so great to see you both," I say after we exchange hugs.

"You, too, Texas," Evelyn says. "And you look amazing. You're glowing. But you also look like you're ready to pop. Are you sure you're okay about tonight?"

"She's the star attraction," Jamie says. "Of course, she'll be there."

I wave the words away. "My part's just a short speech," I say. "You're the one explaining the news. Which is fine," I add with a grin, "since you love the spotlight so much."

"I do," she says. "I really do." She leans back and fluffs her dark hair as she flashes a camera-ready grin. I'm girl-next-door pretty, but Jamie has always had those movie star good looks, and even now that she's no longer the young ingénue, she has a spark that shines on camera.

"Well, both of you will do great tonight," Evelyn assures us. "After all, this project is your baby."

She glances down at my belly again. "Your other baby." She grins. "Speaking of, how are those two little girls?"

"They're doing great." I can feel myself smiling.

Jamie runs her finger over the rim of her wineglass. "Great is an understatement. Those girls are so adorable. Almost makes me want one of my very own." She cocks her head, making a show of thinking, then shakes it. "Actually no. I'm happy to just be able to borrow yours when I feel that maternal urge come on."

One of these days, I'd like to see Jamie and Ryan with a baby. But I have a feeling that day isn't coming any time soon.

"I never thought I wanted kids," Evelyn says. "And honestly, I don't have any regrets. But every once in a while, there's a little ping." She leans across the table and takes my hands. "That's only one of the many reasons I'm happy that you're in my life, Texas. Playing Grandma, I mean."

"There are a lot of reasons I'm happy you're in my life," I say honestly, then make my expression bland. "Babysitting is definitely on the list."

Evelyn chuckles, then lifts her glass of wine in a toast. We clink, and we all drink. Them with their wine and me with sparkling water.

"Speaking of built-in family babysitters," I add, "you and Frank coming together tonight, right?"

Frank is my father, but he left my mother—and me—when I was a child. A few years ago, he re-appeared, and though it was rocky early on, he's now fully in my life again. I even call him Dad on occasion, but I tend to default to Frank around other people. Especially around Evelyn.

They've been dating for a while, and the truth is, if I call him Dad, that makes her Mom. That's not a bad thing. Not at all. After all, my biological mother is a piece of work, and someone who had—at least until this morning—completely disappeared from my life after I firmly kicked her to the curb after years of abuse and harassment.

So with Evelyn, it's not as if I already have a mom I don't want replaced. In fact, it's just the opposite. Evelyn already feels like a mother to me, but since I don't know where this thing with my father is going, I don't want to get my hopes up.

Of course, Evelyn has been in Damien's life since his earliest tennis days, and she's remained a lifelong friend. I know she'll always be around, but I can't deny the fantasy that one day she'll play a bigger role. And, honestly, I can only hope that my father understands what he has in her and has the guts to make it permanent. He might not. After being married to Elizabeth Fairchild, I can definitely imagine that he'd be gun-shy.

I'm saved from my meandering thoughts by the arrival of the waiter, and I order a light chicken salad even though I'm not hungry. Lately, there's barely been enough room in my stomach for food. Jamie orders the burrito plate, but Evelyn sticks with her wine and a side salad.

"I'm saving up for tonight," she says. "Your father and I are going out to dinner before we head to the foundation."

"Perfect," I say, before we move the conversation away from my dad and my pregnancy and on to more mundane catching up. Evelyn has gotten back into agenting, and she shares some great stories about the ridiculous hurdles that she has to jump to navigate Hollywood. And, as a plus, she represents Jamie, and they both gush about a new job that Jamie is up for, apologizing for not being able to give me the details about the hush-hush project.

"I'm just happy something's in the works," I tell them both. "You know me. Hollywood details just *whoosh* right over my head."

"Unless we're talking classic movies," Jamie says sagely. "Then she's all over it."

We all laugh. My lack of knowledge about the business isn't a secret, though I do try to pay attention more since it's now the bread and butter for two of my favorite people. I'm especially happy for Jamie, who's always wanted to be on camera, and is now living her dream, both as an actress and as an on-camera entertainment correspondent.

She's been my best friend since Texas, and though she used to be a wild child piece of work, she's calmed down considerably since she married Damien's best friend and business partner, Ryan Hunter. He's a perfect match for her, since he not only keeps her in check, but he doesn't deny her that bit of wildness that makes Jamie Jamie.

Ryan took over at the Stark Security Agency when Damien founded it after Anne's kidnapping. Thinking about that usually makes me shiver, but I've gotten to the point where I can handle the memories. And I'm so proud of what my husband has accomplished with that organization.

Our conversation continues to meander all over the place in that kind of easy back and forth you have with friends and family.

I rest my hands on my belly as I look at these two women and think about our circle of friends and my husband right there in the center of it.

Yeah, I think, as I sigh happily. It really is all about family.

Chapter Three

*D*amien crossed the tile floor to the table where the three women sat, then stood behind his wife.

"This is what I like to see," he said as Nikki turned in her seat and smiled up at him. "Three of my favorite women enjoying lunch together."

"What on earth are you doing here?" Nikki asked, her pleasure at seeing him coming through in her voice.

He lifted his phone, as if that were answer enough. Apparently it was, because she laughed. "Edward told on me," she said.

"He said you were tired and going home for the day. I told him I'd pick you up. I spent my morning at the Domino, so I was conveniently located to act as chauffeur for my wife."

"Well, I can't say I'm sad to see you," Evelyn said. "You're just lucky you came when we were already done with your wife." She reached over and patted Nikki's hand. "Or, perhaps, she was done with us."

"This has been wonderful, but I can definitely use a nap," Nikki said.

Jamie shook her head. "With all this talk about exhaustion and the other aches and pains that go along with pregnancy, you guys are definitely not talking me into having a kiddo anytime soon." She aimed a bright smile up at Damien. "Fortunately, between you two and Jackson and Sylvia, I'm swimming in nieces and nephews."

He laughed. "Which means, of course, that we can call on you to babysit anytime."

"Absolutely. And so long as I'm not naked and in bed with your best friend, we'll rush right over."

Nikki made a show of holding her hands over her stomach. "Careful. He might hear you."

Jamie waved away the words. "Well, he has to get to know his Aunt Jamie soon, doesn't he?"

"Can't argue with that," Nikki said, reaching out for Damien. He took her hand, wondering what he'd ever done to get so lucky.

"Ladies, I've already taken care of the check. Now I'm going to take care of my wife." He pointed between Evelyn and Jamie's drinks. "You two go ahead and finish up, but if you don't mind I'm going to take her now. I think it's time someone rested."

"Normally I would get on him for handling me," Nikki said, pushing her chair back. "But I really am exhausted. And," she added looking up at Damien with a smile. "I'm very happy with my designated driver."

He watched as she gave both women a hug, then he brushed a kiss over both their cheeks. For a man whose childhood should be listed in the *Guinness Book of World Records* as worst ever, he'd ended up winning the Friends and Family Lottery.

He kept a hand at Nikki's lower back, not only because he enjoyed feeling the way she moved against him, but also because he wanted to be close in case she slipped. His normally graceful wife was definitely lacking in grace these days.

She smiled up at him. "Waddling," she said, then rolled her eyes.

"Yes. But you do it with such pizzazz."

As he'd hoped, she giggled. "So home?" She looked up and down the street then frowned, obviously not seeing his car. "Why didn't you have the valet leave it here if you knew we were coming straight out?"

"To be honest, I lied. I'm happy to take you home if you're too tired, but I thought it might be nice to take a walk on the beach." He was carrying a soft-sided leather briefcase, and he tapped it now. "I brought your Leica," he said. "I'd like to get a shot of you by the water."

She looked between him and the beach. The restaurant was a short walk from the Pier, and they could easily cross the parking lot, then walk through the sand to the water. But walking on the loose sand wasn't easy, and if she was already tired…

For a moment her face was almost unreadable, which was unusual, as Damien had developed the knack of reading Nikki's expressions over the years. Then he saw the answer in her eyes. The bright joy that spread to her mouth, ending in a stunning, brilliant smile. "That sounds wonderful," she said, squeezing his hand. "Thank you for thinking of it."

"It's for both of us," he said, but he was touched by her words. Nikki had been an amateur photographer for years, taking her camera on every trip and even taking lessons from their friend Wyatt Royce, a highly sought-after professional photographer.

But she'd never taken any pictures of herself during her pregnancy with Anne, though they did have some studio shots of him, Lara, and a very pregnant Nikki. They'd taken tons of pictures in China when they got Lara, but the only candid pictures of her pregnancy with Anne were the snaps he'd taken using the camera on his phone.

This time, he wanted to be more deliberate.

"We don't have a tripod, though," she said. "It's not like I can take a selfie."

"I think I can handle it," he said. "You tell me how you want to stage it, and I'll take the picture."

She narrowed her eyes putting the tip of a finger next to her mouth as she made a show of studying him. Then she made a light scoffing sound. "Well, I suppose if you're the best I've got to work with." He laughed, then pulled her close and kissed her. "I love you Mrs. Stark," he said.

"That's very convenient," she said. "Because I love you, too."

He took her hand, and they crossed the street, then he held on even more tightly when they reached the sand, making sure that she didn't trip and fall as the earth moved beneath them. As he'd expected, she regained her footing when they reached the packed sand near the surf.

"Down there," she said, pointing to an area with fewer people, the hills rising in the distance. He understood immediately what she intended, because if he stood at just the right angle, he could get Malibu in the picture behind her.

"I thought about what you said this morning," he told her as they walked hand-in-hand in the surf toward their photo spot. She'd worn slip-ons to work, as had become her habit, and they were now in his case, as were his work shoes. The camera itself was slung over his shoulder.

She kicked her toes a little, and he couldn't help but worry that she would fall. He didn't say anything, though. She'd been through this before, and Anne was born just fine.

"What I said? Oh, you mean about a nanny?"

"Exactly. And as much as Gregory loves those kids, I have to say I think you're right. He should have the privilege of enjoying them, not having them be part of his workload. I want him to be able to kick back and be Grandpa when he wants to."

She turned up her head, looking up at him, her smile so bright he wondered what he could've possibly said. All he'd done was reiterate that she was right.

"What?" He pressed when she said nothing, just continued to smile.

"I love that you called him Grandpa," she said. "They've got Frank, of course, but that's about it. It's not like we're going to be inviting Jeremiah into the fold any time soon."

"No," Damien said, stifling a shiver. The thought that his father would ever step into the role of grandfather to his children came close to making him physically ill.

"I was thinking about it earlier, too," she said. "In the restaurant, I mean."

"Gregory?"

"No, no. About family, and what it means. I was thinking that Evelyn is more or less their grandmother."

Damien chuckled. "And considering how close she and Frank are becoming..."

"I would hip bump you if I didn't think it would make me fall over and topple into the sand," she said with a laugh. "And you're right about that. But even if my dad wasn't in the picture, that's still who she is, you know?"

He did. He and Nikki knew better than anyone that family was about where you found it. Not about blood. He squeezed her hand. "So we're agreed? We'll see if we can find someone to take the burden from Gregory? Even if we can only find someone part time at first."

"Absolutely," Nikki says.

"I'll have Troy call a few services and we can see what kind of availability there is. But we'll talk to him before hiring," Damien said. "I don't want to just spring it on him."

"No, of course not. He's family."

"Exactly. And I think so long as he understands that we're not kicking him to the curb, but hoping that he can enjoy the girls more in his own way, he'll not only agree, but will be happy with the arrangement."

"I hope so," she said. "We can talk to him when we get back."

He shook his head. "Oh no, no. No. I'm taking you home so you can get some rest."

"Damien—"

He tapped a finger to her lips. "No," he said firmly. "The girls are at his house right now watching movies, and he promised them both *The Aristocats* and *Lady and the Tramp*. Then *Finding Nemo* if they're extra good and take a nap."

"In other words, they're there for the rest of the afternoon and into the evening."

"Until morning," Damien said. "Since we're going out anyway, he thought it would be a fun adventure for them to stay at his place."

Her smile was wide. "Well, that's very interesting."

"Oh, no," he said. "You have to make a speech tonight, and you need to rest."

"The funny thing about pregnancy hormones is that I may be tired but I also desperately want my husband." She slid into his arms as if in proof of the concept. And when her hands slipped between them to cup him, he knew she wasn't just teasing. He pulled her close and kissed her gently.

"You're being naughty, Mrs. Stark."

"Only because you like it that way."

He grinned. His wife did know him well. He also knew he had to take care of her and the baby. And that she had an exhausting evening ahead of her. "Come on," he said.

"Home?"

"A photograph," he said, turning her so that he would get the hills and the ocean in the shot. "And as soon as we get the perfect image, I'm taking you home and putting you to bed."

Chapter Four

I'd been exhausted on the beach, but now that we're back in the house, I can't seem to drift off. That's the thing about hormones—they've made me completely wonky, and whatever sleep fairy had been tempting me has completely left the building.

"Oh, no," Damien says, as I start to sit up. "After almost nine months, I know that's a bad idea. You don't want to be dead on your feet at the foundation tonight. Sleep, wife of mine."

I fall back against the pillows, the light down comforter at my waist. I'd changed into a loose, pullover maternity dress as soon as we got home, and I'm still wearing it now, the soft cotton soothing against my skin.

Damien's sitting on the edge of the bed, smiling down at me.

"I'm not much of a napper," I say.

"I know."

"But during pregnancy? All bets are off."

He chuckles. "I know that, too."

I reach for his hand. "But right now—I don't know if I'm

nervous about tonight or if the walk just got my blood flowing, but sleep isn't coming."

"Let's see what we can do about that," he says.

I narrow my eyes. "We?"

"All the way."

"What?" I have no idea what he means.

"Roll over and close your eyes all the way."

"Oh." I lick my lips, wondering what he has in store for me, but I comply and shut my eyes as I roll to my side, the way I've been sleeping for the last few months.

At first, I feel nothing other than his breath against back of my neck and the brush of his pants against my bare legs. Then his fingertips graze my neck as he brushes my hair to the side. Those fingers move to my arm, lightly stroking my skin, as his lips dance over the back of my neck, sending delicious sparks tingling all the way down my spine.

"Damien…"

"Shhh." He doesn't miss a beat as his hand moves from my arm to my hip, then slowly starts to hitch up my skirt. I draw in a breath, making a soft, needy voice in my throat. I'm not wearing panties—they're so constricting and I wanted to be comfortable—and now I'm not sure if I should curse or applaud that decision, because Damien's fingers are now stroking my leg, just above my knee, and the man himself is inching lower and lower in the bed.

I start to open my eyes, but stop when I hear his quick *tsk*. Instead, I bite my lower lip, then draw in another breath when I feel the bed move as he sits up, one hand on my knee that's pressed to the mattress, the other on my hip.

"Roll over, baby," he urges, even as he's gently helping me do exactly that. I've been careful to sleep on my side because I've heard it's better for the baby, and now I make a soft noise of protest as I look at him. He must understand, because he whispers. "It's okay, baby. This won't take long."

There's a fire in his voice. A promise that shoots through

me, and I sigh as he pushes my dress up, then runs his hands lightly over my belly. I close my eyes, both aroused and soothed by his touch, all the more so when he gently spreads my legs and slides up so that his hands are on either side of me and his lips are brushing the tight skin of my belly.

My pulse kicks up as he slowly kisses his way south, his hands moving to my hips, then the juncture of my thighs as his mouth trails over the mountain that is my body. My breath is coming in stutters now, and his kisses are trailing lower and lower. Then his mouth is on my public bone and I gasp, then bite my lower lip as he keeps going, his tongue flicking over my clit.

Electricity zings through me, and I start to squirm, but Damien holds me in place, his tongue and mouth teasing me as wild sensations build inside of me, and though I try to shift, to move just enough to take some of the edge of these pounding, rising, incredible feelings, he isn't letting me. I have to take it all, and I suck in air, my body filling up with something primal and powerful until I can't take it anymore and I cry out as I explode in a shower of brilliant lights and vibrant colors.

"Damien," I murmur, as I finally come back to myself.

"I'm here," he says, moving up the bed, then brushing a kiss on my shoulder. I roll onto my side, then sigh happily as he spoons against me.

"That was…"

"Yes, baby?"

"That was wonderful," I say, the world feeling thick and heavy. "But I think I need that nap now."

And though I hear his soft laughter in my ear, it soon fades, as I'm tugged down into a warm and dreamless sleep.

I'm still basking in the afterglow of both sex and my nap when we pull into the Stark Children's Foundation grounds right on the dot at five. Technically, the event starts at five-thirty, with cocktails and conversation followed by my short announcement and Jamie's longer presentation, but we came early to give us time to wander the grounds and chat with the kids who are actually in residence.

Over the years, Damien has both supported and created several charitable institutions, and this one was one of his first. The SCF is dedicated to helping abused and neglected children find help, homes, and a proper education. Many even live and go to school on site until they find adoptive or foster families. Located on several acres in the Hollywood Hills, the foundation is an incredible organization and one I'm happy to be part of.

I've recently stepped into the role of an SCF Youth Advocate, and I've been dealing primarily with kids who are cutting or otherwise working out their issues through self-harm. It's a good role for me, as God knows I understand that compulsion well. I've always been a cutter—and I know I'll always have to guard against that urge—but it wasn't until after Anne's kidnapping, when I relapsed and took a blade to my skin again, that I publicly said so. It had been a terrifying revelation, but in speaking out and sharing my story, I'd turned a difficult, personal revelation into something good.

We're in the cherry red Bugatti Veyron, one of Damien's favorite cars, and two of the boys who are currently living on-site come rushing over, eager to see inside.

"Just a quick look, Mr. Stark," Joshua, a precocious four-teen-year-old begs.

"Yes, please," adds Allen, who, at twelve, has been Joshua's wingman since they met.

Damien laughs, then holds the door open, letting them take turns sliding behind the wheel. He catches my eye as I circle the hood, then adds a small shrug.

I wiggle my fingers, letting him know it's both okay and expected—what man *could* resist showing off that car?—and start to walk toward the main building so I can look over my notes before I'm behind the podium. I don't get that far, though. I see two more kids, both girls, leaning against the fence post that outlines a field where the foundation's four horses can run free or be saddled for lessons.

Mellie, a pale thirteen-year-old with a mass of red curls, lifts her hand in greetings, but quickly drops her eyes. I frown, then put my speech back into my shoulder bag and veer in her direction.

Tascha, her nine-year-old companion who is beyond shy, takes off running for the residence, but Millie stays put. "I don't want to talk to you," she says when I approach.

Her words aren't harsh, just sad, and they send a warning ricocheting through me. "I'm sorry about that, because I always like talking to you."

She looks up at me, her wide eyes damp. "I was afraid you'd be able to tell."

I force myself not to react, though I want to reach out and touch her and help carry her pain. "No, that's one of the hardest things about it. How secret it can be, so nobody ever knows you need help."

Her chin rises. "I don't need help."

"Don't you?"

We've fallen in step together, and now I sit on a bench, patting the seat beside me. "So what was the trigger?"

She looks up at me blinking away tears. "My mom. What else?"

I put my hand on her shoulder. "Yeah," I say. "I get it."

She meets my eyes and nods. We've talked a lot about my cutting over the last few months, and how my own mother's attitude and expectations affected me. She made me believe I was weak, and it came to a point where I needed to cut to get through most every trauma of my life. I'm past that now, my own resolve pushing me through, and Damian's strong hand at my back helping me to stay steady. But I know how hard it can be, and I know that I will always have to fight that urge.

"How bad?" I ask.

"Hardly at all," she says, her voice small as if that's a bad thing. "I put it here," she says pointing to her inner thigh, the place where I almost always dragged the blade, too.

"It's okay, Mellie."

"Is it?"

"Everybody breaks sometimes," I say, paraphrasing what Damien once told me. "That's why I'm here. To help."

She nods and draws a breath.

"How bad was it?" My voice is carefully level so she doesn't hear the depth of my concern. "Did you have to go to the ER?"

She shakes her head. "No. No, I didn't even draw blood. But I put the knife there. And I wanted to. And then I didn't want to want to."

I draw in a breath my entire body feeling lighter. And then I hold out my arms for her, and she hugs me like she was my own little girl, this thirteen-year-old, who came to the foundation lost and scared two years ago after her mom was convicted of assault, and is now serving time. "Oh, kiddo, don't you know, that's a victory."

"No it's not. I haven't cut in months and months. I haven't even come close. Then I go and visit her because it's her birthday and I figure she'll be okay, but—"

She cuts herself off with a violent shake of her head. I force myself not to speak about her relationship with her mother; that's a tripwire for me, and better suited for her therapist. But I can talk about the result of that encounter, and I make a point of meeting and holding her eyes.

"You need to believe me when I say this was a victory, not a step back."

She snorts, and I can't help but smile.

"It's true. Because whether you like it or not, that's part of you. It's always going to be hard. And sometimes it's going to be really, really hard. But you didn't cut. You beat it back. Don't you see? You won. It was a really hard battle, but you won."

"Really?" She blinks back tears, but one escapes, and she wipes it away. The motion so swift it seems almost angry.

"Yes. Really. Don't you remember when we met? I pretty much told the same story to the world, and you came up to me and told me that I should be proud."

"That's because that's what Annabeth said," she says, referring to her therapist.

I nod. "And Annabeth is right. Do you not believe her?"

Mellie shrugs. "I did. When it was about you. But now it's me, and I just feel like…" She drifts off, shrugging again.

"You feel like you failed."

She nods.

"Well, that's one of the challenges too. Learning to accept the little victories. So let me accept this one for you, okay?" I take both her hands and look hard at her face. "This is a victory. I promise you. So even if you don't believe it yet, will you at least take my word for it?"

"You really think it's a good thing?"

"Honey, anytime you don't cut, it's a good thing. And anytime your mom starts to make you feel that way, you know you can call me. I gave you my number, remember?"

Now she doesn't meet my eyes. "I know, but I didn't want to … I mean you're…" She trails off, indicating my stomach.

I laugh. "I promise you, unless I'm actually in labor, I will take your call. I wouldn't give you the card if I didn't mean it."

She hesitates, then nods. "Thanks, Nikki."

I give her a sideways hug. "Any time. And will you do me a favor?"

Her mouth turns down. "I guess so."

"I have to go make a speech. Will you come with me? I'd really love to have you in my corner."

"Absolutely," she says. "I'll always have your back." We start walking to the center together, and she pulls me to a stop.

"What's wrong?" I ask.

"I just wanted to say, I liked Annabeth, and I think she's a really good therapist. I'm sorry I didn't believe her when she said it was a victory."

"You don't have to be sorry."

"It's just that it's still not easy, and I want it to be."

"I know."

"I know you do and that's why I wanted to talk to you. Because you're so strong. And I know that if you are, then I can be too."

I try very hard to swallow the tears that have gathered in my throat. Because I never thought of myself as strong before Damien, and I don't think I can express to this girl how wonderful it makes me feel to know that I now stand for her the way he does for me.

"I'm glad, Mellie," I manage to say. "I can't tell you how glad that makes me."

Chapter Five

"Gotta hand it to you, Damien. You did good."

Damien turned to see Evelyn standing beside him. She was smiling, and there was a kind of pride in her eyes he'd never seen before. A different pride than what he saw in Nikki, his wife and love, or his brother Jackson, or even from his friends and coworkers. Evelyn was smiling at him like a parent, filling that role she'd silently adopted so many years ago.

He reached for her hand and returned the smile. "Well, you know how much this place means to me. I'm glad it shows." He cast his gaze around the large room where Nikki and Jamie were about to announce the reason for this celebratory cocktail party that the foundation was hosting for its supporters.

She chuckled, then lifted a hand, signaling to someone. Across the room, he saw Frank Dunlop lift his chin in acknowledgment, then start making his way toward them.

"Of course I know," Evelyn continued, and he heard the truth in her voice. She'd been with him during the worst horrors of his childhood. She hadn't known all of the details, but she had known some, and she'd definitely seen the big picture.

She'd been one of the few who had kept his biggest secret over the years, a dark secret, that had haunted him, that he'd never thought he would have the power to overcome, at least not until Nikki had come into his life.

Now, with her, he knew that anything was possible.

He was smiling, thinking of her, as Frank moved in closer and slipped an arm easily around Evelyn's waist.

Damien forced himself not to react or comment. Not to smile, not to hope. But he did hope. For Nikki's sake he hoped that these two people who loved them—and whom he and Nikki loved—were truly together. That Evelyn and Frank's relationship was another brick in the fortress that was the family that they were building, stone by stone, relationship by relationship, friend by friend.

"I know," Evelyn repeated, "but it's not the foundation that I was talking about."

Damien cocked his head, eyeing her with surprise. "No?"

She shook her head. "I'm talking about Nikki," she said gently, nodding to where his wife stood by the stage, ready to climb the steps to the podium. "I'm talking about how good she is for you. How good you are for each other."

Damien swallowed, moved by her words.

"I don't know if I somehow knew what you two would be to each other that day I met her on my patio," Evelyn continued. "But I'm going to say that I did. Might as well take credit where credit isn't due." She flashed him a wicked grin. "Isn't that the Hollywood way?"

Damien laughed, catching Frank's eye as the older man grinned. From what he'd seen, Frank cared about Hollywood as much as his daughter did—as in, not at all— but he cared completely about Evelyn, and as far as Damien was concerned that was the true measure of the man.

Damien reached out for Evelyn's hand, then squeezed it. "I'm not going to argue with a word you've said."

"Good. Plus, you know how proud I am of Nikki for what she's done here, too."

"I know," he said sincerely. "Me, too." He'd been hesitant

when Nikki first told him that she wanted to become a youth advocate at the foundation. They'd still been so close to coming out the other side of the horror of Anne's kidnapping—so close to when she'd once again taken a blade to her skin.

His heart had broken for her, but he understood. Hell, at the time she'd cut, everything felt as though it was falling apart, and God knew he'd been hanging on by a thread himself. When you got right down to it, the only difference was he'd beaten himself up with fists and fury, whereas his wife had turned to the steel of a blade.

He'd understood, sure. But he'd also feared that she was too raw to take on the pain of these kids as well, and when she'd told him she wanted to publicly discuss her cutting and work with the kids as a Youth Advocate, he couldn't help but worry.

Now, of course, he knew that Nikki had made the right choice. He'd seen her with the kids, and he knew damn well that this was something she was born to do. He glanced around the room and saw Mellie, the teen who had come to them broken and scared, and who now had so much confidence and laughter in her eyes.

Mellie saw him looking at her, then rolled her eyes as she cocked her head, then pressed a finger over her lips before pointing to the podium, as if to tell him to be quiet, idiot, his wife was about to speak. He grinned in acknowledgment, then turned to look at his wife.

For years, he'd been telling her that she was strong, and there had never been a day when he didn't believe it. But today he saw it fully. She looked powerful as she stood up there, as in-control as he'd ever been in a boardroom. His wife, his love. The woman he would give his life for, and the woman he admired more than anyone else in this world.

"That's it," Evelyn whispered beside him. "That look in your eye right now. That's the kind of pride I have for both of you."

He swallowed moved by her words, and he squeezed her

hand in silent acknowledgement as Nikki began to speak. Her voice was strong, and she made eye contact with several members of the audience, just as he'd been taught by all the PR people who used to circle him back in his tennis days.

He'd seen her speak before, both at functions like this and to potential clients and partners. More than that, he knew that she'd had training. She'd been forced into various pageants that her mother had made her enter. It had been her own personal hell—he knew that—he couldn't deny that she'd walked out of that experience poised and articulate, and he supposed in a way, she'd turned something horrible into something good. Like a diamond out of coal.

"—and that's why we're taking today to honor you, our volunteers and donors," Nikki said, well into her speech by now. An acknowledgment of all the people who donated their time and money to help the kids that the SCF sponsored. "Please, give yourself a round of applause."

She met Damien's eyes as he clapped with the rest of the crowd, then smiled. "But this isn't just a day to celebrate what we already have," she continued as the applause died down. "We have something special in the works, and it's my honor to announce to you all that starting next month we'll begin filming for a documentary series that follows the journey of several of the kids who've been the recipients of aid from the Stark Children's Foundation or scholarships from the Stark Education Foundation. We have so many wonderful—I—I mean, so many wonderful stories to tell, and…"

Damien frowned as she continued, only half-listening as she talked about the series that had recently been green-lit. As far as he could tell, he was the only person in the audience who had even noticed the hitch.

But he *had* noticed, and it wasn't a simple stumble of words. He knew her too well. And even now he heard the tremor in her voice as she said, "A-and now I'll turn the microphone over to our producer, Jamie Archer Hunter, who—, um, who can give you more details and answer your questions."

Damien frowned, still concerned, and he barely noticed as Jamie approached the podium as Nikki stepped away. He barely noticed, because his eyes were searching the room, and stiffened when he saw what had made Nikki stumble.

Elizabeth Fairchild, Nikki's mother, standing right in the doorway.

Chapter Six

$\mathcal{I}$ keep my eyes on Mellie as I finish my speech. I *want* to find Damien in the crowd. Want his strength to fuel my own. But I keep my focus on Mellie because I have to. Because I *can*. Because I told her I'm strong, and dammit, I am.

There is no way I'm standing up here and letting her see my weakness betray me. If anything, I'm going to be the proof that it's possible to fight your demons.

All of which is good and well, I think as I descend from the stage, but what the hell is my mother doing here, anyway?

I draw in a breath and paste on a smile as I quickly introduce Jamie. Her smile is equally wide, but I know her well enough to see the question in her eyes. I'm not fooling her at all. More than that, I hear the quick little intake of breath as she casts her gaze out over the audience, obviously catching the coiffed blond-gray hair of my mother.

She turns back to me, and for what seems like an eternity but is surely only a brief moment, our eyes meet and hold. Then she pastes on her camera-ready smile, reaches for my hand, gives me a quick squeeze for solidarity, and says, "Let's all give Nikki Stark a round of applause. She was instrumental in bringing this program to life, not to mention all the work she does here at the Stark Children's Foundation."

I nod my head in acknowledgement, then quickly descend from the platform, taking care to hold the handrail. Not because I'm unsteady because of my pregnancy, but because my mother has knocked me completely off-kilter.

I'm not surprised to find Damien waiting for me just a few feet away. When I'd been on the podium, he'd been standing in the center of the room, right in the middle of my focus. I don't know how he's gotten to me so quickly—the room is packed—but he's there, right where I need him.

He pulls me into a tight hug, telling me in a voice loud enough for anybody standing nearby to hear, that he's so proud of me and the work I've been doing as a Youth Advocate and in getting the docuseries off the ground.

All of that is true, of course, but what he's really saying is that he's proud of me for not losing it at the unexpected sight of Elizabeth Fairchild.

We slip off to the side, knowing that no one is going to judge us harshly for leaving while Jamie is providing more information about the upcoming series. As soon as we're out of the main area and in one of the halls, Damien reaches out and tucks a lock of hair behind my ear. "Are you okay?" he asks, his eyes hard on mine.

I nod. "I'm fine."

He studies me, then extends his hand. "Maybe we haven't met..."

I laugh. I used that same line on him once when he was bullshitting me.

"I'm surprised," I admit. "And she definitely knocked me off my game. But I guess I'm okay. I'm just kicking myself, because I should have confronted her. I should have shown myself and Mellie that I'm strong."

"You are strong," Damien says. "And you confronted her before. Kicked her very squarely back to Texas, as I recall."

That's true. I had. And I was damned proud of myself, too. I still am. But that doesn't answer the big question—why the hell isn't she still halfway across the country?

"I don't get it," I say. "She has to know she's not welcome."

"No," Damien says. "She's not welcome at all."

As I watch, he pulls out his phone and taps out a message. He doesn't say what he's doing, but I'm certain I know, and I take a step backward so that I can see out into the main area from where we are in the hallway.

Jamie is still speaking, showing slides of some of the kids who will be featured in the first episodes, and the audience is rapt. As she speaks, I see two security guards move towards my mother. I watch, amazed and thrilled, as Elizabeth Fairchild is escorted off the premises, her eyes going wide as she passes my father in the process.

I press my hand over my mouth to hide a smile as I see my mother's eyes widen in recognition. Her mouth drops open, but she doesn't get a word out before the security guards have led her away, removing the interloper from this exclusive, ticketed event.

As soon as she's out of sight and out of the main building, Frank and Evelyn join us in the hall. Immediately, I fold myself into Evelyn's warm embrace. "I'm proud of you, Texas," she says.

I grin up at her, my brows raised. "For managing to not lose my shit, you mean?"

"Damn right," she says, and we all laugh together.

"I'm sorry," Frank says, and I think how perfect those simple words are as he pulls me into a hug.

That's the moment that every bit of doubt is erased. The moment that I know how right it was to let him back into my life, and that no matter what mistakes he made, this man is my father again.

But over the years, I've also learned a hard truth—that Elizabeth Fairchild is never stepping into that role again. For that matter, she was never really a mother to me. Not in the sense of what that word really means.

And as I hold my husband's hand and lean against Evelyn, all I can think is how grateful I am for the people in my life who really do love me.

∿

"The kids are gone," Damien says, "and I believe that I promised you a long, lazy night of making love."

I sigh and snuggle closer to my husband. We're on the couch, my head in his lap, and I've been randomly flipping through channels, bouncing back and forth between various streaming services, looking for something that strikes our fancy. "That sounds wonderful," I say, setting the remote beside me on the cushion.

He gently turns my head, so he can look at me more directly. "I think I hear a but," he says, and I have to laugh. He knows me so well.

"I like this," I say. "This lazy moment of just being with you, on the couch, maybe watching TV, maybe talking, maybe reading." I reach up and brush my fingers over his beard stubble as he strokes my hair.

"Are you saying that you're turning down sex with me for a long, lazy night just sitting here talking with me?"

I grin. "Shocking, I know, but do you mind?"

He chuckles. "Baby, you know there's nothing I would rather do than spend time with you. Do you want to pick a show?"

I move my head back and forth, feeling lazy. "If there's something you want to watch, I'm up for it. Otherwise, I'm happy to just sit here, maybe talking, maybe just listening to you flip through the magazines you're trying to catch up on." I'd seen the stack when we'd come into the living area, a huge pile of various engineering and science-related reading material, which is not only Damien's jam, but a key part of how he stays on top of his industry.

He laughs. "Busted."

"Go ahead," I say. "I'm happy just being here."

His fingers slide through my hair once again, then he picks up a magazine and puts it in his lap. I feel the brush of the pages against my hair every time he turns one.

I close my eyes, enjoying the moment. This lazy time, where everything can just drift away. Not the good things—those are surrounding me, keeping me warm and safe. My husband. The kids nearby at Gregory's house. The warm embrace of our home.

I relish the way this moment acts as a barrier against the cold, hard thoughts that had bothered me earlier this evening. That nagging question of why my mother is back in town and what the hell she wants.

I don't know the answer, and that uncertainty bothers me. But being with Damien like this—knowing that I'm truly loved—makes all of that wondering bearable.

I draw in a breath and let my eyes flutter open as I look at his gorgeous face. He smiles at me, then presses a kiss to his fingertips and gently brushes them over my lips.

"I love you, baby," he says.

"Yes," I tell him. "I know."

Chapter Seven

"*M*ommy! Guess what, Mommy!" The words greet me as I step into the kitchen area. "Mr. G's taking us on a nature hike!"

I glance over at Gregory who lifts his shoulders in a hint of shrug. I hide my smile, and turn my attention back to Lara. "And where are you going on this nature hike?"

"Between our house and Mr. G's," she says. "We're exavating."

I fight a smile. "Are you really?"

Gregory hides his own smile behind a hand as Anne pipes up and adds, "We're very 'portant."

Lara nods. "We're gonna collect the rocks and flowers and stuff, but we're looking for the best position, too."

"Position for what?" I ask.

"The secret room," Anne says, her eyes going wide.

I do my best not to laugh. "Wow. That really is cool. I'm impressed Mr. Gregory has asked you two to help him with that very important project. You'll do a good job, right?"

They both nod solemnly, and I shoot Gregory a wink even as I wonder what location they're going to come up with.

The Malibu house was originally intended to have a wine

cellar as a sub-basement, but the builders ran into some sort of trouble during construction. That was all before Damien and I were together, and I never did ask Damien what exactly the problem was.

Recently, though, he's gotten into collecting wine, and we've decided to build a cellar on the property. The goal is for it to be accessed from the house if possible, but if the engineering of that won't work, it will simply have a hidden door in the hills, much like Damien's twenty-car, Bat cave-like garage does.

"I thought it would be fun for the girls to get out and look at the land. Of course, Mr. Steele will make the final decision as to location, but I told Mr. Stark that I'd come up with a few preliminary options."

"Sounds good to me," I say, wishing that Gregory would call us by our first names, but knowing he never will. As for Mr. Steele, that's Damien's brother, Jackson, and he's designing the cellar for us, since building wine caves does not fall within Damien's varied skillsets. Or mine, either. Jackson, however, is a world-renowned architect. As far as I'm concerned, we're lucky to have him in the family.

"The girls will enjoy getting a closer look at the rocks and plant life," he adds. "We'll end the day with some sort of craft project using whatever they collect."

"You are so great with them," I tell him honestly. "But are you sure you want to set them free in the wild? They'll run you ragged." We have a lot of property. And while the girls will—I think—behave, I can just imagine how much they could wear Gregory out.

He flashes a grandfatherly smile. "Don't worry about me. I can handle it. And Mr. Steele will be arriving in less than an hour."

"Will he?" I look to Anne and Lara. "Does that mean your cousins are coming today?" They both nod, looking giddy. Ronnie and Jeffery are not only cousins, but also best friends with our two, and the four kids always have an incredible time when they're together.

"Ms. Lee said that they could stay for our lesson, too," Lara says.

"Mommy, look! I drew Dory!" Anne pipes in from where she's once again seated at the kid-size table.

Lara crosses her arms. "Anne, I was talking."

Anne looks abashed. I go over and put my hand on her shoulder. "It's okay, sweetie. You're not in trouble, but your sister's right. We don't interrupt."

"But—" I press a finger to my lip, and she silences with a huff.

"That's fine if they stay," I tell Lara. "But that doesn't mean you get to just play during your lesson."

"I know, Mommy." Ms. Lee is their Mandarin teacher who's been teaching the girls for about a year now. Damien and I don't know if Lara will ever want to visit China or explore her heritage in any meaningful way, but we also want her to have the option, and understand the language of the country in which she was born. And, of course, Anne's joining her in the endeavor.

I turn my attention back to Anne, and look down at her paper. "Wow. That's a beautiful Dory," I say, referring to her wildly colorful and somewhat scribbly rendition of the Pixar fish.

She beams up at me then hands me the sheet of paper. "It's for you, Mommy."

I feel my heart squeeze a little. "Really? I love it. Can I take it to the office with me and put it on the wall?" She nods happily, then slides out of her chair to give me a hug. I squeeze her back, then draw Lara in too.

"I wish I could go on the walk with my girls today, but I have to go to work. I have things to get finished before your baby brother comes."

They both put their hands on my tummy, then Lara shifts to put her ear there. "He's still not talking."

"He's probably overwhelmed by you two, and doesn't know what to say."

They both laugh, and I bend down to kiss them goodbye. Then I look at Gregory, mouth *thank you*, and head off to start my workday.

~

"So we'll go with Amelia, Franco, and Jennifer," Eric says, pulling up each resume in turn off my desk and putting it into the leather portfolio he's holding on his lap.

"You're in charge," I say from where I'm sitting behind my desk. "If those are your choices, then those are the choices."

He narrows his eyes and shifts in the guest chair. "Are you saying you don't like my choices?"

I laugh. "Eric, you're sharp, and you know what you're doing. Don't second-guess yourself."

He frowns, then taps the portfolio. "No, you're right. Those are the best candidates. I have a few on my second tier, too," he adds, "but hopefully we'll find our perfect person after I interview the first round."

"Let me know if you want me to be available when you do the interviews. Like I said, you're perfectly capable of doing it on your own, but if you do it soon enough, I can be here in case you need moral support."

"Thanks. I'll see what their availability is, but I may start the interviews tomorrow if I can get at least one of them in here."

I nod. "Then we're all good. Anything else?"

"Maybe. Hang on." He opens his portfolio and starts to page through some loose sheets, but before he finds what he's looking for there's a tap on the doorjamb. The door itself is wide open, and I look up to see Bree Bernstein standing right there, her long dark hair pulled up in a bouncy ponytail and a smile in her stunning, deep-set eyes.

"Bree!" I push back and rush to her with considerably less grace than the last time she saw me. We hug, and I push back with a grin. "What on earth are you doing here? You're supposed to be in New York."

"I've been here for a couple of days, actually," she says, then looks me up and down. "You look so great. I can't wait to meet the new little Stark."

"You and me both," I say, and we laugh.

"Great to see you again, Bree," Eric says, before excusing himself to go call the candidates.

I gesture to a chair. "Please," I say. "I'm dying to catch up. Can you come to the house? The kids would love to see you. Are you here for a vacation? I wish you'd told me, we would have planned something."

She laughs, obviously not able to catch up with my rambling, then shakes her head. "I would love to come by, and we'll make sure to arrange a time. I'm only here for a few days, though. I'm in town with my mom looking for an apartment."

"An apartment?" I frown. "What happened to New York?"

Bree had moved to Manhattan to pursue a journalism degree. She'd been a huge part of our family before that, although there had been some decidedly rough patches in the midst of the kidnapping crisis. So rough, in fact, that Damien had given her a studio condo along with a trust to cover costs.

Now, she looks a little abashed. "To be honest, the program wasn't a good fit. I'm doing a low residency program in fiction now—I'm working on a novel—and, well, I just wanted to be in LA. I'm, um, sorry about the studio."

"Are you kidding? It's yours, remember? Rent it, sell it, do what you want with it."

She visibly relaxes. "Thanks," she says. "And I do want to see the girls. Maybe tomorrow? Right now I really just popped in to tell you about me moving back. And to introduce you to my mom. She's only staying for the day. She's catching a red eye back. I asked Marge to give me a sec and then bring her back."

"I'd love to meet her." I move back behind my desk and sit, gesturing for her to take one of the two guest chairs. I reach over and buzz Marge, but since there's no answer I presume she's on her way, a belief that's supported when I hear footsteps approaching my office.

I stand, expecting to see Mrs. Bernstein, who I've only seen pictures of.

But it's not Bree's mother who crosses my threshold.

I take a step back, holding onto my credenza and forcing myself not to fall into my office chair. "Mother, I … what on earth are you doing here?"

Chapter Eight

"*M*other." I have to clear my throat. I can barely speak. "What—what are you doing here?"

She takes a single step into my office, and I tense. "I wanted to see my daughter, of course." She looks around the room, a trademark Elizabeth Fairchild smile plastered across her face. "There's nothing wrong with that, is there?"

"But how did you get in here?" I want to scream that *of course* there's something wrong with that. That *of course* I don't want her here, and just by being in this building, she's tainted the whole damn day.

Instead I manage to pull myself together and say, "You just strolled into my office because you *wanted* to? Who does that?"

"I heard your voice," she says, "so how could I resist? And I assumed you wouldn't mind. I'm your mother, after all, and I—"

"Excuse me!" Marge's sharp voice rings out down the hall. I hear footsteps, then see the woman herself in the doorway, looking more harried than usual. She shoots me an apologetic look, then scowls at my mother. "Ma'am, I asked you to wait in the reception area."

She turns her attention back to me, shaking her head. "Ms.

Fairchild, I'm so sorry. This woman said that she was your mother, and I asked her to wait. I was bringing Bree's mother back, and we stopped at the ladies room. I intended to tell you she was here and ask if you wanted me to check her driver's license, but now—"

I hold up a hand, seeing how frazzled she is. Beside her, Bree's mother slips into the room, shooting me an apologetic glance as she goes to Bree's side, then holds her daughter's hand.

"It's okay, Marge," I say. "Believe me. I know how hard it is to control my mother." I shoot a glare towards my mother, then look back at Marge again. "Really. It's fine. You can go back to the front. I'll buzz you if I need anything."

Marge looks like she's about to argue, but then she turns and disappears down the hall, but not before narrowing her eyes at my mother. Marge rules the reception area with a firm hand, and anyone who breaks those rules is immediately on her bad side.

My mother straightens her back and sniffs, paying no attention to Marge, her eyes only on me. "I'm your mother, Nichole. I should have certain privileges."

"It's Nikki," I say, plastering on my most polite smile. "And you have no privileges at all." I'm certain she expects me not to draw attention to our estrangement. That is how a polite young lady would behave, after all.

Of course, she's wrong. I glance over at Bree and her mother, holding hands in familial solidarity. I don't have that. And I will never have that, not with Elizabeth Fairchild, anyway. But just seeing them together, makes me more empowered. More certain of the relationship I want with my own children.

I roll my shoulders back, look my mother in the eyes, and say very clearly, "I need you to leave."

Instead of snapping out a criticism, she surprises me by dipping her eyes down, as if in remorse or apology. When she lifts her head, I can't read my mother's face. It's as smooth as glass. "I'm sorry to get off on the wrong foot," she says simply. "The truth is I came because I wanted to thank you."

I shift my weight, feeling unbalanced and ungainly, and not just because of the pregnancy.

"I know that when we last met, I wasn't the woman I should have been. I wasn't the mother you needed or the grandmother I could be." She's been holding a shopping bag, and now she sets it on the ground between us, as if presenting some sort of gift to a monarch.

"These are for your little girls. And I would love to sit down and have the chance to talk with you. To see them. You've done so much for me, you and your husband. The house, the bank account. I know I never said how much I appreciate it, but of course I do. And I would very much like to meet the girls."

I draw a breath, trying to stay calm. Her voice sounds so even, so reasonable. And yet I don't trust it. I can't trust it.

But oh, God, I want to trust it....

"No."

I practically bark the word, the sound surprising me as much as her. I reach out for my desk, suddenly unsteady on my feet, and I'm not sure if it's because of my mother's presence or lightheadedness because of my pregnancy.

I take a step backwards and sit in the chair. Bree and her mother are still standing on the other side of my desk, and I see Bree's brow furrow, concern painted on her face. On her mother's as well.

My mother's face remains unreadable.

"Please," my mother says. "I'm in town with a friend from Dallas, but I will make whatever time you want for me. I so very much want to ease back into your life. I know I made mistakes, Nichole. I was so scared of being poor when I was younger, and the truth is I'm so grateful to you and to Damien for everything you've done for me."

She looks toward Bree and smiles. "I'm so glad you've built friendships here in Los Angeles. That you have a good life now.

And perhaps I should just leave you to it, but well, the truth is that I'm a grandmother now. I never thought I would be, but I am. And I would really like to learn how to be a good one."

I'm not sure if I want to laugh or to cry. If I want to pull her into a hug or push her hard away. All my life, she's been a manipulative bitch, and I can't believe that she's changed so quickly. And yet….

And yet, she's saying all the right things.

I need time, I know that. I need time to think. To not react rashly. To not push her away because of all the horrible years between us, and to not pull her close because she puts on a good show.

I close my eyes, and I count to three. And when I open them again, I feel stronger. "I'm sorry," I say, "but no."

I expect her temper. I expect her to tell me I'm the ungrateful little bitch I've always been. Instead, she inclines her head, and says, very softly, "I understand."

And then to my surprise, she turns and leaves.

Chapter Nine

"No way," Jamie says, her voice coming through Coop's sound system loud and clear. "No way in hell is your mother sincere. Not unless she had a personality transplant, and the last time I flipped through the pages of a medical journal, that still wasn't something they could do."

Despite the topic, I can't help but laugh. I called her from the office before leaving, but she hadn't gotten back to me until I was already almost home, and now I'm maneuvering my beloved Mini Cooper past the gatehouse. I wave at Gus, the guard on duty today, and continue toward the circular driveway in front of our door.

I kill the engine, then stay in the car for a while, talking to her now through the speaker on my phone. "I know," I say. "I know all of that. And yet…."

"I get it," she says again. "I mean I don't completely get it, because my mother is a human, but I still get it."

I smirk. She's really not wrong.

"What does Damien say?"

"I haven't told him yet," I confess. "I knew that he had back-to-back meetings today, and you know Damien."

"Yeah," Jamie says, which is enough. I know she understands that I didn't want him to rearrange his entire schedule in order to make sure that the reappearance of my mother wasn't messing with my head.

"I'm home now, though," I say. "I'll talk to him in a bit."

"Is he home?"

"Not sure. He wasn't planning on coming home early today, but he might be." Damien often rides in with Edward so that he can get work done in the back while Edward's driving. And if he drives himself, it's usually because he's taking one of his toys, in which case he parks in the bat cave, and walks into the house through the underground tunnel.

"Well, hugs," she says. "And stay strong. I know you want your mother to magically turn into a human, but the odds are against it."

I laugh. "I know. But, hey, I won the lottery with Damien. Miracles do happen."

"Not twice in one lifetime."

I say nothing. She's probably right about that. My rational side is warring with my emotional side, and my emotional side is all hyped up because of my hormones. I know this. I just can't seem to convince myself that I know it and push my mother out of my mind.

"Hey," Jamie says gently. "I wish I was there to give you a real hug. I know it's got to be hell. I don't mean to make light of it."

I wish she were here for a hug as well. "I know," I say. "Love you, James."

"Love you back, Nicholas."

I get out of the car, and head into the house, bolstered by Jamie's pep talk. I step inside, then come to a dead stop when I find Damien and my father sitting on the couch in the first floor living area.

Since we're hardly ever down here unless we're hosting a pool party, I narrow my eyes at both of them. "Okay. I'll bite. What's up?"

Damien's brows rise, and guilt crashes over me. Honestly, by now I should know better than to try and keep anything from this man, even if for only a few minutes.

"I knew you had meetings all day," I tell him truthfully. "I figured I'd tell you when I got home."

"She came to your office?" Frank asks. "She actually walked into your office?"

I frown, then settle into a chair opposite them. "Marge, right? She's the snitch."

Damien's mouth twitches just enough that I know he's not mad—but he was genuinely worried. Considering the ways in which I've melted down around my mother in the past, I suppose that's fair.

"Bree, actually," Damien says.

"She called you? I was going to tell you when I got home that she's probably coming over tomorrow. The girls are going to be so excited."

"Already on the calendar," he says with a little smile toward Frank. I look between the two of them. "What aren't you telling me?"

Damien scowls, but I see the humor in his eyes. "Not anything more than you're not telling me."

I cross my arms. "Damien…."

"Apparently, Bree is moving back to Los Angeles."

"She told me. Something about a low residency writing program."

"Right," he says. "She called to apologize about living in the condo. I explained to her that it's hers to do with as she wishes. Apparently you'd already told her the same, and she said she was glad we felt that way as she was planning to rent the condo and use the income for rent here."

"Okay." I'm not sure where this is going, but he seems to be coming to a point.

"I told her it was silly not to save that money if she could. She could use it for her tuition or even invest it."

"Sure, if she lives on the street." I tilt my head. "Wait a second…" The pieces are starting to fall together. "Damien? What are you getting at?"

"Bree needs time to write and a place to stay. We need a nanny. I'm very good at math," he adds with a grin, "and I worked that equation out all by myself."

"You're serious?" I'm absolutely delighted.

"I am. Bree's coming back to be our nanny again while she works on her novel and finishes her MFA program. Technically, she'll be full-time, but when she needs a break, we all know that Gregory is there to fill the gap."

I would throw my arms around him, but there's no way I can get out of this chair fast enough. So instead I just clap, absolutely thrilled. "I wish I'd thought of that myself."

"I didn't think you would object, so I went ahead and offered her the position. I hope that's okay."

"Are you kidding? I just told you. It's amazing." I look over at Frank. "Isn't he the best?"

My father laughs. "Yes. I couldn't have asked for better for my little girl." His face darkens, and I know that we're shifting the conversation now. "Of course, I suppose you could have done better on the parent side of things."

That's worth pushing out of my chair, and I do, then go and sit beside him. "I did just fine on the paternal side of things," I tell him as I take his hand. "A bit of a rocky start, maybe, but it's smooth now. You know that's how I feel, right?"

"I do." He draws a breath. "Now my fear is that you feel the same way about your mother."

I sink back into the cushion as Damien moves to sit on the coffee table, so that he's directly in front of me. I look between the two of them and shrug. "I don't want to," I say honestly. "And I really don't. Trust her, I mean." I take a long, deep breath. "But I am second-guessing myself. She seemed so sincere. What if I'm wrong and she really does want to make amends?"

"Even if she does," Damien says, "and to be clear, I don't believe it at all. But even if she does, you don't have to accept the apology or open our life to her. She made her bed."

"I know," I say, wishing I wasn't a walking mass of hormones so I could think more clearly. "I really do know. I just feel … weepy," I finally say. "I just want to curl up and cry about all the lost potential."

"Sweetheart," Frank says, giving my hand a squeeze. "I understand that. After all, we both know how much I screwed up, and you let me back in. It makes sense that you're wondering if you should do the same with your mother."

I nod, because it's exactly that. What I don't know is whether I should act on that.

"I don't think you should," he continues. "But I also don't think I'm in a position to help you make that call."

"I am," Damien says firmly, then he leans forward and takes my hand. "I don't want to see you hurt again."

I draw in a deep breath. "And I don't want to be." I glance at Frank, then back to Damien. "But don't people deserve second chances?"

I'm thinking out loud, still not sure what I believe, but not wanting to make a misstep in something so important.

"I mean, think about Sofia," I continue, looking into Damien's eyes.

I see the amber one fire with regret. The dark one with loss. "Nikki…"

"No." I reach for his hand. "I mean it. Think about how many chances you gave her." He'd grown up with Sofia, a disturbed young woman, who had very much had it in for me. "In the end, she really did do the right thing," I remind him. "Despite everything, she ended up doing the right thing."

"She did," he agrees, "but I always knew her heart. I always knew that she loved me. But baby, your mother … baby, I'm not sure she's capable."

I swallow. He's not wrong. Even so, I say, "Maybe she's

trying." But even as I speak the words, I know they're not true. I've known my whole life that I was nothing more than a doll to my mother. Something pretty and malleable she could dress up and bend to her liking.

"I can't trust her," Damien says. "But if this is what you want, then we can let her back into our life."

I draw in a breath, surprised he'd agree to that after everything she's put us through. But at the same time, I'm not surprised. After all, Damien loves me, and I know he'll support me. He'll also protect me. Because God knows if I let her back into my life, everything might come crashing down around me again. And it will be Damien who picks up the pieces.

I look at Frank, who is obviously working very hard to keep his expression bland. I know that he feels the same as Damien. He doesn't trust my mother either. And although I know he believes that he once stood in the same position as my mother, that's not actually the truth.

Frank left my mother, not me and my sister. He loved us. But by leaving us behind with Mother, he believes he failed us. In a way, he did, but it wasn't because of lack of love; it was because of his own insecurities and incompetence. Things that he's now acknowledged and is trying to make amends for.

Is my mother trying to make amends?

The truth is, I don't believe it. As much as I want to, I didn't hear sincerity in her voice. At the same time, though, I don't want to be wrong, and I so desperately want my children to have grandparents.

But then I look at Frank. I think about Evelyn. I think about Jackson and Sylvia and their kids, and all our friends.

My children have love—so much love—and that's something that I never had. Why would I open the door to a woman like my mother, and expect her to love her grandkids when she never even loved her own daughter?

I take Damien's hand. "No," I say, firmly, certain the decision is the right one. "Elizabeth Fairchild isn't welcome here."

Chapter Ten

"What if we put a tower right here?" Damien said, taking a green LEGO Duplo block and stacking it on top of a red one.

They were in the first floor playroom, him on the floor with the girls, Nikki parked in a chair at the little table scattered with children's books and toys. He grinned up at her. "You know, if the girls and I make this big enough, it could fill the whole room. We wouldn't have to buy a playhouse."

She laughed. "I think you're delving into your brother's territory." She cocked her head, frowning as she studied the building or castle or fort or whatever it was that he and his girls were putting together. "I think Frank Lloyd Wright is probably turning over in his grave right now."

"Honestly? I wouldn't doubt it."

Anne called for him, and he started to turn toward his youngest, but he paused when he heard Nikki wince. He started to rise, but she lifted a hand and waved him back down.

"I'm just uncomfortable. Only time will fix that," she added, patting her belly. "Just a few more weeks. That's what I keep reminding myself. Are you listening in there?" she said, bending her head to talk to their son. "Don't make Mommy wait, okay?"

"You know," Damien said, "I've read that S-E-X sometimes gets labor started. We could give it a shot. I'm all about being helpful."

"Yeah, I bet you are." Laughter colored her voice. "But if that's really true, then this baby should have been born one month after conception." She batted her eyes at him. "And I don't think my math is off at all."

"Well, you might have a point there." He pushed himself up to his feet, went to her, then very soundly kissed his wife. "Fortunately we didn't induce premature labor, despite our very best efforts...."

She rolled her eyes, then pointed across the room. "Go. Build a city with your children. I'm going to sit here and rub this goo on my tummy." She had a tube of coconut scented moisturizing cream that she'd been rubbing on her belly, and now she leaned back, lifting her shirt a bit and sighing as she started to rub it in.

Damien had just dropped down to the floor next to Lara, who was very carefully stacking blocks, when Nikki's phone rang. He glanced over out of habit as she pressed the button for the speaker, mouthing *Jamie*. "Hey, what's up?"

"Am I on speaker? Are the girls there?"

"Auntie Jamie, Auntie Jamie!" Both Lara and Anne stood and jumped and ran towards the phone. "Are you coming over? Hi, Auntie Jamie."

"Hey, girls! I'll see you guys soon, okay? I just called to talk to your mom for a minute. Okay? I love you."

"Love you too! Love you!" both girls shouted at their aunt, then hurried back to Damien and the business of building.

"So what's going on?" Nikki asked. "My hands are gooey, so you're still on speaker."

"I was calling to see how you were doing after the whole situation with your M-O-M."

Nikki laughed. "You Know Who knows how to spell that word, you know," she said, referring to Lara who was reading far above her age level. "But she's also busy doing something else at the moment."

She met Damien's eyes as she glanced towards their eldest. Sure enough, the little girl was busy drawing on a pad of paper, apparently designing the next wing of their building. Or possibly drawing a horse. He wasn't entirely sure.

"Right," Jamie said. "Damn they grow up fast. Oh, shit, I'm on speaker aren't I? I shouldn't have said damn. Or shit. *Oh, shit.*"

Now Nikki really was about to laugh, and Damien didn't blame her.

"Okay," Jamie said. "Trying again. I just wanted to ask you what you were going to do. Did you decide?"

"I did," Nikki said. "I don't know what I was thinking even hesitating for a moment. I know who she is. I know who she'll never be. And I don't want her around my kids."

For a moment Damien heard nothing. Then he heard Jamie's *phew!*

Nikki's brows rose. "Okay. What gives? That's more than relief that I made the right decision."

"Honestly I hesitate to even tell you, especially since your husband is in the room, and I don't want to be an accessory before the fact."

"Jamie…" He made sure the warning was clear in his voice.

"All right, all right. Just remember, you don't have to actually *do* anything about it."

"Do anything about what?"

"I decided to do a little poking around. She told you that she came to town with somebody, right? Somebody from Dallas?"

"Yeah," Nikki said. "A friend."

"Nope. Not a friend. The woman lives in Dallas now, but that's only temporary. She's a producer on one of those reality shows that follow local celebrities. Apparently your mother is hustling for a spot, wanting to get in as the mother-in-law of

Damien Stark. But she wants to be on your good side, because who wants to be the woman that Nikki and Damien Stark shunned?"

"Oh!" Nikki made a low grunting sound, and Damien almost laughed at the way she cut off what must have been a curse so the children wouldn't notice.

Other than that though, he wasn't laughing.

At the same time, he wasn't surprised. He certainly wouldn't put anything like that past Elizabeth Fairchild.

"I knew it," Nikki said. "I mean I didn't know it, of course, but I should have guessed. And everything you're telling me confirms what I've already decided. That woman isn't part of our life anymore. Whatever strings were left, are now completely snipped."

"Good," Jamie said, echoing Damien's thoughts. "Because as far as I'm concerned you've had more than enough of that woman in your life. You don't need her."

"No," Nikki agreed. "I don't need her at all."

"I'm going to come over and see the girls tomorrow, okay? You'll tell them."

Damien saw Nikki look over at them to see if they had acknowledged that they were being talked about, but they were both deep into coloring now.

"I'll tell them," Nikki said. "They'll be thrilled to play with Aunt Jamie. Beware that they're currently in a LEGO kind of mood. You'll probably be building the pyramids or something."

"I can get behind that," Jamie said. "Although I thought we might make a little movie."

"Lara would absolutely love that. She can play director and editor. And Anne can be their star."

Or their gopher, thought Damien. Though he knew that with either job, Anne would be in heaven, too.

He tuned the women out as they finished their conversation, his attention turning back to his children, so much so that he didn't even realize they'd ended the call until Nikki's phone rang again. She hit the speaker button once more, and this time it was Gus, the front gate guard, whose voice filled the room.

"Mrs. Stark," he began, "there's a woman here asking to enter the property. She says she's your mother."

Damien started to rise off the ground, but Nikki shook her head and put her hand out. "Would you mind handing her the phone?" Nikki said, and he heard Gus' confused, "Well, sure," followed by Elizabeth's smooth, "Nikki, darling, your guard apparently needs assurance that I am who I say I am."

"Mother, you are exactly who you say you are. But as far as I'm concerned you're not part of this family. I'm sorry you drove all the way to Malibu. For that matter I'm sorry you came all the way to California. But I think it's time for you to go home now."

"Nikki, this is your mother you're speaking to. I have a right to see my grandchildren."

"The hell you do. You don't have any rights at all where they're concerned," Nikki said. She started to reach for the phone as if she was going to stand and go into another room, but then she settled back in the chair again, her face contorted with what he assumed was anger. "You need to just go, Mother."

"I absolutely will not."

"Yes," she said. "It's time—" She drew in a sharp breath. "Mother, just go. It's time."

And then she ended the call abruptly, her eyes cutting straight to Damien's. "Damien," she said, her voice laced with excitement. "It's time."

For a moment he just sat there, not sure what she meant. Then it hit him, and he felt that mixture of terror and excitement. That same mashup of raw emotions he hadn't felt since Anne was born.

"Right," he said, and despite having gone to the mat on more billion-dollar deals than he could recall off hand, in that moment he forgot everything on the checklist they'd had ready for months.

He drew a breath, dredged up the memory of what he was supposed to do, and met his wife's amused eyes.

In a few minutes—when the next contraction hit—he knew that expression wouldn't be so warm.

He lifted his wrist, looking at his watch face. "Okay, okay we need to time the contractions and get you to the hospital."

"No."

He looked up, frowning at her. "What? Am I forgetting something? I'll call Gregory for the girls, Edward for the car. Your bag's by the door."

"No," she said, breathing hard and bending over in pain as she clutched the table.

He felt panic rise. She shouldn't be having another contraction so soon.

"They're coming too fast," she said when it subsided, confirming his fear. "Way faster than Anne. Call Dr. Albright. Damien, call him now."

After that, everything was a blur. The doctor agreed that she didn't have time to get to the hospital. For that matter she didn't really have time to get upstairs to the bed.

Instead Damien had Gregory get the girls out of the room as Damien converted the playroom's sleeper sofa into a bed. The contractions were coming about two minutes apart, and Damien was a wreck as he managed to get Nikki onto the bed and settled.

He held her hand through the contractions as she crushed his fingers and cried out that they were coming too fast, that this wasn't right, that something had to be wrong.

He soothed and consoled, but he had the same fear. She'd been in labor all night with Anne. This wasn't going how he had imagined, and he was terrified that his son was in distress and the damn paramedics hadn't arrived yet. Damien had done a lot of things in his life, but delivering a child was not among them.

Time seemed to crawl, but it was really only minutes before the EMTs arrived, escorted in by Gregory, who hurried back out again quickly. Damien barely noticed. All he could focus on was Nikki, helping her through the pain, and praying that their son was fine despite things moving so damn fast, his poor wife drenched in sweat and crying in pain.

Finally, the female paramedic, Jenny, told him to hold one of Nikki's legs as she held the other to help Nikki bear down, and then—*oh God, how had that happened? How had he actually been a participant in that happening?*—he saw the top of his son's little head.

And then the boy was there in the world. And before Damien could even catch his breath, the paramedic was putting the baby on Nikki, and Damien was cutting the cord with a shaking hand, as Jenny smiled and congratulated him.

He had a son. He had a wife, two beautiful daughters, and a son who kept his own timetable and had one hell of a set of lungs. Dear God, how did he deserve this?

Nikki smiled, her eyes drooping. "He's perfect," she whispered, her voice going straight to his soul.

"Yes," Damien said, holding her hand. "You both are."

Epilogue

*T*he morning sun streams through the window as I sit propped up in bed with my son sleeping in my arms. He's just been fed, and although I'd hoped he'd stay awake for his Grandpa and "Evie," as Evelyn wants to be called, he's completely conked out.

They've left now to take the girls down to the beach, and it's just me and Damien and our son in my arms.

Damien sits beside me. "He came early, the rascal."

"Like his daddy, he has a mind of his own."

"I hope so," Damien says, and so do I.

"Do you want to hold him?"

"He's falling asleep. I don't want to disturb him."

"You won't," I assure him, shifting my arms so that I can pass our precious bundle to his daddy.

"Hey there," Damien says, once the baby's settled in his arms. "He's gorgeous. Just like you."

I shake my head. "He's obscenely handsome. Like you."

Damien grins, then shakes his head. "No. He's his own man."

"Baby Boy Stark," I say, as Damien cups his son's tiny head. "We're going to have to do better than that."

"He's strong," Damien says, his voice full of pride.

"Like his daddy. Nothing's getting the better of our little man."

"He's a fighter. He needs a name that reflects that."

"Yes," I coo, to my son. "That's exactly what my baby boy needs." I glance up at Damien. "Does Daddy have any ideas?"

Damien starts to shake his head, then I see the light bulb flicker behind those dual-colored eyes. "As a matter of fact, Daddy has the perfect name."

"Tell me," I say, then tap my ear. "Whisper it." I don't want our baby hearing his name until we're certain. Superstitious, maybe, but I think that's allowed.

Damien leans forward, looking pleased with himself, and when he tells me the name, I have to agree that he has reason to be. "Yes," I say, then pull him down for a kiss before returning my attention back to our son. "That's an absolutely perfect name."

THE END

HELP NAME BABY BOY STARK!

Curious to know the B.B.S.'s name? You'll find out in Enchant Me!

And more than that, **you** *have a say in what Nikki and Damien name the baby!*

Just type in the link below to submit your choice for Baby Boy Stark's name, then be sure to pre-order **Enchant Me** *so you're the first to know his name!*

Here's the link:

https://www.juliekenner.com/lets-name-baby-boy-stark/

(All readers who submit the chosen name will receive an acknowledgment in the book!)

Hurry, the suggestion form will be closed at midnight CST on May 31, 2021!

More Nikki & Damien....

It was supposed to be a new beginning for billionaire Damien Stark, his wife Nikki, and their family…

I thought I knew everything about my beloved husband, Damien Stark. In our years together, I'd heard all the rumors, faced all the dark secrets, and survived the danger that comes hand-in-hand with loving a powerful magnate like Damien.

After all we've been through, I believed we were finally free of the past, of the darkness, ready to move into the light of our future together. As we stand ready to renew our vows in front of our friends and family and move on to the next chapter of our life together, I am giddy with joy and love.

I am unprepared for the devastation that steals my happiness and threatens our future in ways I never imagined. Given our past, I should have expected it. But how could I when Damien didn't either?

This man has come from nowhere, and he says he's Damien's son. Everything is chaos, Damien is wrecked, and I don't know where to turn. The worst part? I think I believe him.

And he has promised to destroy everything we love.

Be sure to grab *ENCHANT ME*

~

*A*nd keep reading for the first FOUR chapters of *My Fallen Saint*, the first book in my newest trilogy featuring billionaire philanthropist Devlin Saint.

"Something unimaginable and extraordinary has happened in My Fallen Saint. Devlin Saint just captured my heart's number one spot as a broken, dominating and delicious alpha man from J. Kenner. This story was explosive and enticing. It was such a powerful mix of passion, suspense and angst. I have no words. No words." *PP's Bookshelf*

My Fallen Saint

EXCERPT

CHAPTER ONE

The wind stings my face and the glare from the afternoon sun obscures my vision as I fly down the long stretch of Sunset Canyon Road at well over a hundred miles per hour.

My heart pounds and my palms are sweaty, but not because of my speed. On the contrary, this is what I need. The rush. The thrill. I crave it like a junkie, and it affects me like a toddler on a sugar high.

Honestly, it's taking every ounce of my willpower not to put my 1965 Shelby Cobra through her paces and kick her powerful engine up even more.

I can't, though. Not today. Not here.

Not when I'm back, and certainly not when my home-coming has roused a swarm of butterflies in my stomach. When every curve in this road brings back memories that have tears clogging my throat and my bowels rumbling with nerves.

Dammit.

I pound down the clutch, then slam my foot onto the brake, shifting into neutral as I simultaneously yank the wheel sharply to the left. The tires squeal in protest as I make a U-turn across the oncoming lane, the car's ass fishtailing before skidding to a stop in the turnout. I'm breathing hard, and honestly, I think Shelby is, too. She's more than a car to me; she's a lifelong best friend, and I don't usually fuck with her like this.

Now, though…

Well, now she's dangerously close to the cliff's edge, her entire passenger side resting parallel to a void that boasts a view of the distant coastline. Not to mention a seriously stunning glimpse of the small downtown below.

I ratchet up the emergency brake as my heartbeat pounds in my throat. And only when I'm certain we won't go skidding down the side of the cliff do I kill Shelby's engine, wipe my sweaty palms on my jeans, and let my body relax.

Well, hello to you, too, Laguna Cortez.

With a sigh, I take off my ball cap, allowing my dark curls to bounce free around my face and graze my shoulders.

"Get a grip, Ellie," I murmur, then suck in a deep breath. Not so much for courage—I'm not afraid of this town—but for fortitude. Because Laguna Cortez beat me down before, and it's going to take all of my strength to walk those streets again.

One more breath, and then I step out of the car. I walk to the edge of the turnout. There's no barrier, and loose dirt and small stones clatter down the hill as I balance on the very edge.

Below me, jagged rocks protrude from the canyon walls. Further down, the harsh angles smooth to gentle slopes with homes of all shapes and sizes nestled among the rocks and scrubby plants. The tiled roofs follow the tightly winding road that leads down to the Arts District. Tucked neatly in the valley formed by a U of hills and canyons, the area opens onto the town's largest beach and draws a steady stream of tourists and locals.

As far as the public is concerned, Laguna Cortez is one of the gems of the Pacific Coast. A laid-back town with just under sixty-thousand people and miles of sandy and rocky beaches.

Most people would give their right arm to live here.

As far as I'm concerned, it's hell.

It's the place where I lost my heart and my virginity. Not to mention everybody close to me. My parents. My uncle.

And Alex.

The boy I'd loved. The man who broke me.

Not a single one of them is here anymore. My family, all dead. And Alex, long gone.

I ran, too, desperate to escape the weight of my losses and the sting of betrayal. I swore to myself that I'd never return.

As far as I was concerned, nothing would get me back.

But now it's ten years later, and here am I again, drawn back down to hell by the ghosts of my past.

CHAPTER TWO

I met Alex Leto on my sixteenth birthday, and the first time I saw him, something inside me turned on. Something like happiness, yet so much more complicated. Optimism, maybe, but mixed with rainbows and unicorns.

The day started gray and dismal, with storms rolling in at dawn. They parked themselves over my house, spread their dark gray arms, and stirred up wind and rain from daybreak all the way into the evening. Six of my ten invited guests called to cancel, but even before the party started, I'd known that it was ruined.

I should have seen it coming. Maybe not a gale, but something. After all, I was not the most blessed of kids. For starters, I was an orphan.

I'd turned four the day after my mother died, and though I used to tell my dad that I remembered her, by the time I was ten, that was a lie.

Her brother, my Uncle Peter, moved his commercial real estate business to Laguna Cortez after she died. My dad couldn't afford to hire help, and as Chief of Police he had an erratic schedule. Daddy and I lived in the hills, but I'd go to

Uncle Peter's huge, light-filled beach house most days after school.

It was a stunning home, but I hated every moment away from my dad. Maybe some part of me knew what was coming. I don't know. All I know is that I wanted him beside me and safe.

But wanting doesn't matter. It never does. Wants are just so much fluff, and Fate is a goddamn bitch. The summer I turned thirteen, I learned that lesson well.

That's when a gunman murdered my father, then killed himself. People tried to comfort me by pointing out that my father died on duty in the job he loved. But it didn't help. He was still horribly, painfully dead.

After that, my life spiraled even more. I moved in with Uncle Peter, and all my friends thought that I was so lucky, because there aren't that many beachfront homes in Laguna Cortez.

But I wasn't. I wasn't lucky at all.

Eventually, I grew accustomed to my new normal. I'd find myself going entire days feeling happy, only to hate myself at night, because how could I experience joy when my parents had both died so horribly?

Which was why I wasn't surprised when the storms rolled in on my birthday, because life will always sneak up and bite you.

Still, even with only a few kids showing up, we'd had fun. Instead of the beach, we settled into the media room to watch movies. And when Brandy and I went downstairs to ask Uncle Peter if my favorite pizza place was delivering in the storm, there *he* was.

A few years older than me, Alex was tall and lean, with close-cropped blond hair, a clean-shaven face that still had a boyish roundness, but an expression that was fully adult. His sandy brown eyes held me in place when he turned to look at me. And when his wide mouth curved into a friendly smile, a low, thrum teased between my thighs.

I'd had a crush or two by then, but I'd never reacted that

viscerally to a guy. But Alex … well, a mere glimpse gave me more understanding of what all the fuss was about than any of the late-night gossip sessions at Brandy's frequent slumber parties.

When he came over to shake my hand and wish me a happy birthday, I almost passed out. I was so flustered that I could only stand there, my hand in his, as I tried to play back the conversation of the last few seconds.

Alex Leto. That's how he'd introduced himself. And he was working for Uncle Peter during his gap year while he decided on a college.

"Hi," I'd squeaked, then kicked myself for being utterly uninteresting.

"Trouble with the movie?" Uncle Peter had asked, and I'd squinted at him, not understanding a word. "The projector," he clarified. "Did you come down because I need to fix something?"

"Oh! Right. Pizza. We want to order pizza. Will they deliver in this weather?"

"If not, I can go get it for you," Alex said, and if I hadn't already fallen hard, that would have sealed the deal. A real live Prince Charming right in my kitchen.

Once Uncle Peter agreed, there'd been no more reason to hang out in the kitchen, and Brandy and I reluctantly went back to the media room. "Oh. My. God," she whisper-squealed as we climbed the stairs. "Did you see the way he was looking at you?"

"He was being polite," I countered, though her words revived that down low tingle, now complemented by a swarm of butterflies in my belly.

"Was he?" She winked at me, and I grabbed her wrist before she could burst into the media room.

"Don't say anything."

"What? Why not?"

"I just … I … please? Can we tell them about the pizza and leave it at that?"

"Yeah." She shrugged. "Yeah, sure. If that's what you want."

"Thanks."

She gave me a quick conspiratorial smile. "But he really is super cute."

"I know, right?" And we both burst into giggles, only to fall into total hysterics when our friend Carrie pushed open the door with a scowl.

"Hello? Waiting the movie on you two. I mean, rude."

We clapped our hands over our mouths to bite back another flood of laughter, took our seats, and settled in until the pizza came. And even though Alex was the one who delivered it—and even though he stayed to watch the second half of *Aliens* and sat right next to me—Brandy never said a word. Not then. Not ever.

Which is a big part of why she's my best friend to this day.

After that, Alex was around a lot. Peter had a home office, but he did most of his work at construction sites or in the offices of the apartments and hotels he owned. He'd hired Alex to do administrative stuff, which meant that Alex was at the house most every day.

I turned down beach and movie offers from my friends, choosing to stay in and fetch Alex water and snacks and coffee. Each time I'd linger a bit, asking what he was doing, and he'd never blow me off. He'd even invite me to stay. Then one day he asked if I wanted to help.

"Not as interesting as spending the summer with your friends," he'd said, "but I'd love the company." He smiled then, and that tiny little motion—nothing more than muscles around lips—had melted me.

"Good. Because I'd rather be here."

"Would you?"

I nodded, my heart pounding with such ferocity I was sure he must be able to hear it.

"That works out great, because I like having you here."

I met his eyes, and something deep inside me roared. For the first time in my life, I felt the hard punch of true, sexual desire.

"Right." I swallowed, trying to overcome my desert-dry mouth.

So that's what I did, helping him when I could, taking up space the rest of the time. And we talked. About anything and everything. I'd never been as comfortable with anyone in all my life, and that was despite the humming, buzzing, crackling in the air whenever we were near each other.

"Have you done anything?" Brandy asked when we were back in school months later.

"No! He works for my uncle, remember? Besides, he's eighteen. Me, sixteen. And he knows it."

She waved away my words. "Yeah, but so what? You act older. Ever since … well, my mom says you raised yourself."

Honestly, Mrs. Bradshaw wasn't wrong. My uncle may have sheltered and fed and clothed me these last few years, but that was about it. Nurturing, I got at Brandy's house. And the rest? Well, I guess maybe I did raise myself.

"Eighteen," I repeated firmly. "Nineteen next week."

"That's perfect." Her blue eyes twinkled. "Wrap yourself in a bow, and you can be his present."

I didn't give myself to him, of course, but when he turned nineteen, I gave him a leather friendship bracelet with a Celtic knot. "That's called a love knot," he said, and I felt my cheeks burn hot.

"I—I didn't know."

"Didn't you? Well, it makes it all the more special to me."

"Oh."

He held out his arm to me. "Fasten it?"

I did, lightly stroking my thumb over his wrist as I manipulated the clasp.

"This is fucked up," he said, so soft I could barely hear him.

"What?"

"Us," he said, the words like ice.

"I'm sorry. I should—" I turned to go, but he grabbed my arm and pulled me back. We were alone in Uncle Peter's study, and he held me in place.

"You're sixteen." He practically growled the words. "Why the hell are you only sixteen?"

I shook my head, blinking as I tried to prevent the flood of tears.

"We can't," he said, and I didn't have to ask what he meant.

"I know," I whispered. I'd been talking to the ground, but I told myself that wasn't fair. He deserved the words. He deserved to see my heart. I looked up and met his eyes. "But I want to."

His head tilted in the slightest of nods. "I know," he said. "I want it, too."

CHAPTER THREE

For months, being with Alex was both torture and bliss. It was like living in a pressure cooker, and I think we both knew that the day would come when we couldn't fight it anymore.

Then, right after Christmas break, Brandy's dad pulled up stakes and moved the whole family to San Diego with barely any notice at all. We'd been devastated, and the day before she left, I helped her pack her room and stayed until her mom said I had to go because the movers were coming at five in the morning. I'd left reluctantly, fighting back tears so that Brandy wouldn't lose it all over again.

I got home to find Alex waiting up for me, ostensibly catching up on Uncle Peter's paperwork. I'd hurried up to my room, unable to even talk to him without risking more tears.

I'd been about to doze off when I heard the light tap at my door. I propped myself up, assuming it was Uncle Peter coming to say goodnight. Instead, it was Alex.

He shut the door behind him, then stood on the far side of the room. "I wanted to make sure you're okay."

"I'm sad," I admitted, and it was as if the words were permission for the tears to flow. "I don't think I've been this sad since Daddy died."

"Oh, Ellie…" I barely registered the fact that he'd crossed the room to me. That he was sitting on the edge of the bed, and I was upright and clutching him, sobbing against his shoulder.

I don't know when he slid into bed next to me, but he did. We were both fully clothed, him in jeans and me in PJs, and he held me tight as I snuggled against him. He stroked my hair, and I cried myself to sleep. Not only because Brandy was gone, but because I knew that one day soon, Alex would leave for college, and I'd lose him as well.

Nothing happened that night. Nothing sexual, anyway. But emotionally? Well, whatever bit of my heart I'd held back was fully his by morning. He snuck out before Uncle Peter arrived, and we shared a secret smile in the kitchen as I made toast to eat on the way to school. Just a normal day. Except it would never be normal again.

After that, every day held smiles and shared glances, and I floated on a cloud knowing this wonderful guy had become my rock. Someone solid and real in a world where everyone I loved kept getting ripped away.

I didn't have a party on my seventeenth birthday. With Brandy gone and Alex out of town for some work thing, I couldn't muster the enthusiasm. Instead, Uncle Peter took me out to dinner, and when he went out later that night, I took a twilight stroll down the beach to the tidal pools.

I sat on the rocks, careful not to slip into the pool and disturb the tiny ecosystem. The moon was full, so there was enough light to see the silver fish, brown anemones, and all the rest of the sea life that lived in that fragile little world.

I was bent forward, watching a hermit crab navigate its way across the pool, when I heard the soft pad of footsteps behind me. A spike of fear shot through me, and I jumped to my feet, not even thinking, and lost my footing. I started to go down, certain I'd either squash all the critters in the pool or scrape every bit of exposed skin on the rocks.

But then suddenly I wasn't falling. I was flying, being pulled off the rocks and into Alex's arms.

"I've got you," he said as my blood pounded in my ears. Not from my near miss, but from his proximity. From the sensation of his body pressed against mine as he held my upper arms tight in his clenched hands.

Our eyes met, and though I've never considered myself particularly bold, I moved first, tugging my arms free so I could wrap them around his neck as I rose on my toes and closed my mouth over his.

There was no fear, no worry that he'd push me away. I'd known in the instant before our lips met that this was the way it had to be. This perfect, intense moment that ignited a firestorm inside me as he cupped the back of my neck, pulling me closer until I felt like I could crawl inside of him.

"Ellie," he murmured when we broke apart, and hearing my name on his lips was like throwing gasoline on a fire. I wanted him. All of him. And once again, I lifted myself onto my toes and lost myself in the taste of him.

He hesitated only a moment, but in those few seconds, I feared he'd push me away. But then he made a low noise in his throat and thoroughly claimed my mouth, his tongue tasting and teasing, dancing with mine as his hands slid down to cup my ass.

He pulled me close to him, and I moaned when I felt his erection against my belly. I'd never been this close to a guy, and the proof that he wanted me that way burned inside me, making my inner thighs ache and my core throb.

Then suddenly he wasn't cupping my rear anymore. He had one hand down the back of my shorts and I was spreading my legs, offering him all of me.

"Please," I begged, gasping for air. I wasn't even sure what I was asking for. His finger? His cock? Did I want him to lay me down in the sand and make love to me? Did I want him to take me home?

All I knew was that the answer was *yes*. All I wanted in that moment was to be his, however and wherever he wanted.

When he looked down at me—when I saw the wild, raw heat in his eyes, I knew that's what he craved, too.

This was happening. Oh, God, this was really happening.

But then something in his face shifted, and he pulled his hand out of my shorts. I heard myself whimper as he took a step back, breaking the contact between us.

"Alex?" I heard fear in my voice. Fear that he didn't want me. Fear that I'd done something wrong.

"We can't," he said, taking my hand and holding it close to his chest. "I've never wanted anyone as much as I want you, Ellie. But we can't do this."

I tried to swallow, but the knot of tears stuck in my throat. And when I asked *why* my voice was little more than a croak.

He cupped my cheek. "You're barely seventeen, El. And I'm almost twenty. Plus, I work for your uncle." Something in his face hardened. "Your uncle's not the kind of man who would overlook it. We've already been playing with fire. Push this, and we'll both get burned."

I wanted to shout back that I didn't care. I wanted to burn. I wanted to get lost in the flames with him until we were both reduced to ashes.

But I didn't say any of that because I knew he was right.

He shook his head slowly, his expression profoundly sad. "I never wanted—"

"What?"

"Here. I never wanted to come here."

"To Laguna Cortez?" My voice rose in surprise. "I thought everybody wanted to come here."

"My dad made me. Now, though… " He trailed off, running his fingers over his short hair. "God, Ellie, now this is exactly where I want to be."

"Please," I said, blurting out the word before I lost my nerve. "I want to."

The corner of his mouth curved up. "Me, too. Obviously. But we can't."

"Yes, we can. Uncle Peter's barely noticed that we're friends, much less that there's more."

"Fine. We can."

For a moment, my heart stopped, but then he continued.

"But, El," he said. "I won't."

He stuck to that, too.

Every night, I'd go to bed and slide my hand between my legs while I imagined him doing all the things I read in romance novels. Every night, I'd silently pray for him to sneak into my room and into my bed.

But he never did. He kept his word, even though each time we were alone the air was so charged, I was sure that one of us would crack.

We didn't, though.

Not then. Not yet.

For the next two months, our friendship grew even stronger. Especially with Brandy gone, he became my closest friend. We talked for hours that summer after he was done with work, mostly at the tidal pools. Sometimes he'd stay late at the house, because Uncle Peter was hardly ever home.

We'd talk or cook dinner or watch movies. Horror mostly, because it was an excuse to sit close and hold hands at the first scary scene.

And always, *always*, there was that greedy, guilty need that had me squeezing my thighs to relieve the pressure. I imagined crawling into his lap and doing exactly what the girls in those movies were doing.

And I didn't even care that if I did them, then surely the monster would get me, too.

Maybe I should have cared more. Maybe in the end, I really did bring the monsters down on me.

I don't know. But I vividly remember that September day when Chief Randall came to school and delivered the news that Uncle Peter was dead. Killed by a single bullet to the back of the head, shot from the gun of a monster.

In grief and fear, I'd run home, expecting to find Alex working in the office. But he wasn't there. Later, I learned that he'd been checking the books at one of Uncle Peter's properties when a detective had come to give him the news. They'd questioned Alex for over an hour, digging deep into Uncle Peter's business, searching for clues as to who might have held a grudge.

I didn't know any of that at the time. All I knew was that I was dying inside. That I needed to hear his voice in order to know that he was truly okay. Because everybody I loved—*everybody*—was taken from me. Over and over and over again.

All afternoon and evening I sat with my phone beside me, curled up under a blanket in the living room with Amy Randall, the Chief's wife, bringing me hot tea and cookies. I loved her for taking care of me, but even with Amy in the room, I felt alone.

Alex never called, and at ten o'clock Amy kissed my cheek and got herself settled in the guest room. I went upstairs to my room—and there he was, sitting on the edge of my bed.

I don't know how, but I managed to shut and lock the door behind me before I fell, sobbing, into his arms. "You're going to be okay," Alex whispered. "I hate that you're hurting, but you're strong, El. Never forget how strong you are."

There was an unfamiliar edge to his voice, and he spoke straight to my soul when he said, "I've seen your heart, and you will survive this. And I'll tell you something else, too. I love you, Elsa Holmes." His voice burned with emotion. "That's why I call you El," he added, his thumb and forefinger making the sign for the letter L. "Because it's the first letter in *love*."

Pure joy battled the loss and pain inside me as he cupped

my cheek, his eyes locked on mine. "Promise me you won't ever forget that."

"Alex... " I could barely say his name though my tears.

"Promise me." The words were harsh. Demanding.

"I promise."

He closed his eyes, then took a deep breath. And when he opened them again, I gasped at the wild intensity I saw. The blatant hunger. "Tonight, Ellie. Damn me all to hell, but I've got to have you tonight."

"Yes," I said, though I wanted to cry with relief. "Yes," I repeated, only to have the word lost in the soft brush of his lips, that innocent, tender touch exploding into something much more passionate. Something raw.

Something wonderful.

He flipped me onto my back and straddled me, his mouth hard on mine as I clenched at his hips and pulled him down, craving a deeper connection. Needing skin on skin. I wanted everything I'd been fantasizing about, and I wanted it right then. But at the same time, I wanted this to go slow. To last forever. I wanted no one but Alex, and nothing except being in his arms.

"Ellie," he whispered, then trailed kisses down my neck and lower still. I wasn't wearing a bra, and his mouth closed over my breast through my T-shirt. I arched up, so startled by the intensity of the sensation that I had to bite the soft spot at the base of my thumb in order to keep from crying out. Amy was all the way on the other side of the house and a floor below us, but considering the magnitude of what I was feeling, if I let go, I was certain that my cries of pleasure would shake every wall in the place.

He moved lower then, his tongue teasing the thin strip of bare skin between my shirt and my PJ bottoms, making me writhe beneath him. I felt the brush of his fingers as he unfastened the string, then watched as he lifted his head to meet my eyes while he gently eased my pants down, along with my panties. A shiver ran through me—not fear, but anticipation and wild nerves.

"Okay?"

I nodded, then closed my eyes as he kissed my belly button, then moved slowly lower. His hands were cupped at my sides, his thumbs barely touching the swell of my breasts. The only truly intimate contact was his mouth. Such a small bit of skin to generate such incredible sensations.

He moved with wicked slowness. He probably wanted to make sure I was ready, but I was flying from the heat of him, from the wildness and need he was setting loose inside me. Even with all the times I'd made my own body explode, I'd never experienced this growing anticipation or the pure erotic pleasure of being tended and led down a sensual path toward an avalanche of pleasure.

It almost became too much. I whimpered, then shifted my hips as his lips pressed against my mound. He slid his hands lower, then gripped my waist, holding me firmly in place. Only once did he take his mouth from my skin, and that was when he spoke to me. My eyes were closed, my back arched as my body strained for more. "You should touch yourself," he said. "Your breasts. Your nipples."

"Why?"

"You'll like it," he said. "I will, too."

I swallowed, the thought that he'd watch as I did something so intimate making me more than a little nervous. Ironic, considering how intimately *he* was touching me. But I did as he asked, barely grazing my fingertip over my very tight nipple. And oh my God, the sparks that set off. I closed my eyes again, forgetting to be nervous, letting my hands tease my breasts as his mouth explored below, his tongue flicking over me in ways that had me biting my lower lip to prevent me moaning so much that he'd worry about me and stop.

And then—oh God, and then—my whole body tightened and exploded with way, way, way more intensity than I'd ever managed on my own, because on my own, I'd always stopped. But Alex was relentless, teasing and sucking until I didn't care about embarrassing myself, and I writhed and moaned and screamed until he finally slid up my body, put his hand on my mouth, and reminded me that the walls were thin.

He'd held me then, taking over the job of playing with my breasts, then helping me out of my bunched-up T-shirt so that I was naked and he was still fully dressed.

I bit my lower lip and asked, "Do you want…?" I held my breath, waiting for him to answer. I was warm and sated, but I still wanted more. I wanted *him*.

"Desperately," he said. "I want everything with you, El. I want a night that neither of us will ever forget. I want to bury myself inside you and feel it as you shatter around me." He kissed me gently. "Is that okay?"

I nodded, mute, and he kissed me again before sitting up and reaching for his back pocket. He pulled out his wallet and took out a condom, and I felt like an idiot, then, because I was so worked up it hadn't even occurred to me.

"You've done this before," I said, a bit accusatorially, but that was only to hide my embarrassment.

"No," he said as he peeled off his jeans and shirt.

I rolled my eyes. "I'm not naive, you know."

His smile was both teasing and sweet. "Sex, yes. But never with someone I love."

"Oh."

"I do love you, El, and it's destroying my reason."

I frowned. "What do you mean?"

"We shouldn't do this. Not tonight. Not when I—Not after —But dammit, I want you too much. I can't stand the thought that I might—"

"What?"

"Lose you?"

He made the words a question, and I nodded in under-standing. Peter was the first person he'd lost. And I understood grief better than anyone. "You won't lose me, Alex," I promised. "How can you if we love each other?"

I thought I saw tears in his eyes, but then he kissed me, and once again I was lost as he swept me away, out to sea on a tide of passion. He moved slowly, every touch bringing me that much closer to begging until, finally, I did exactly that and showered him with pleas.

He didn't ask if I was sure—he knew that I was—but he met my eyes, and when he grinned, he was more than my new lover, he was my best friend. And I knew right then that no matter what, the night was going to be perfect.

He buried himself inside me, moving slowly, taking care to hurt me as little as possible, until I was actually whimpering with need. And when he exploded, I opened my eyes and watched the release play out over his face and body, amazed that I had the power to take him there—and then amazed again a few minutes later when he once more sent me off on the same journey until we were both utterly spent and limp as rags.

He slid up the bed, pulling me against him, and we clung to each other, whispering softly until sleep claimed us. I drifted off in his arms, knowing that I would survive this. Because with Alex by my side, I could survive anything.

That's what I believed, anyway, but I learned soon enough that it was a crock of steaming bullshit.

Because by the time I got up the next morning, Alex was gone, vanished with no word other than one crappy slip of paper telling me he was sorry and that I was strong. I'd loved him. I'd trusted him. And he'd walked away.

Everyone else in my life had been stolen from me. But Alex? He'd left of his own accord.

And that made him the worst devil of all.

CHAPTER FOUR

It's Uncle Peter's murder that's dragged me back to Laguna

Cortez. At the time, the police believed the perp was a guy named Ricky Mercado, who'd lost his shit after Peter called him out for dealing drugs at one of the apartment complexes Peter owned.

They believed it because Ricky Mercado turned himself in the day after the murder, and the evidence backed him up. He ended up with a sentence of twenty-five to life, lasted about a decade in prison, then was killed in a prison fight last month.

Just shy of a week ago, I learned from Chief Randall that new evidence shows that Mercado couldn't have committed the crime. Turns out he was in Long Beach at the time of the murder—caught on camera beating the shit out of a clerk at a local convenience store.

So who did kill my uncle? And why the hell did Mercado confess to a crime he didn't commit?

I don't know. But I came back to find out.

My cell phone rings, and I return from the cliff's edge to Shelby. I see that the call's from my editor, so I bend over and grab the phone off the passenger seat. "Hey, Roger. Checking up on me?"

"Checking in on you. How're you doing, kid?"

With anyone else, the nickname would grate on me, but Roger's been my mentor since the first day I arrived at *The Spall Monthly* as an intern after quitting my job with the Irvine Police Department to start a new life in New York as an investigative reporter.

Now I've got a Masters in Journalism and a job as a staff writer, but he's still my mentor and friend. And a little bit of a father, too.

"It's weird being back," I confess, because I know he's worried about me. He doesn't know my entire story, but he knows how my family's ghosts haunt this town. And he knows I'd left Laguna Cortez in my rearview mirror about five minutes after I got my GED during the first semester of what would have been my senior year.

I'd packed five boxes into Shelby, gotten an apartment in Irvine, then worked as a barista until I could start college at UCI in January. I was still seventeen, but Chief Randall and Amy signed off as my court-appointed guardians.

I haven't been back to Laguna Cortez since. I'm not sure I'd be back now if Roger hadn't pushed me.

"Deep breaths," he says. "I've watched you for three years and there's nothing you can't handle."

I cringe. I hate seeming weak, and I'm convinced that's how he saw my reluctance to return. "I've got this," I say firmly. "But I may not turn it into a story."

I pace in front of Shelby, as if moving will ward off the creeping anxiety that's nipping at my heels. "I want to know what really happened to my uncle. But that doesn't mean I want *Spall* publishing it. It's still my life. My family. You get that, right?"

I know he does. But I can't seem to pass up any opportunity to remind him.

"I want you to have closure, Ellie. If that means writing a story, then write it. If it means finding the truth and locking it away, then that's your choice. I won't push you. Not for this story. But you damn well better turn the profile piece in on time."

Now I laugh, because Roger truly is a clever bastard. "I'm on my way to the interview right now," I assure him.

My last argument against coming back was that I had work to do in New York. So my devious editor assigned me to write a profile of the Devlin Saint Foundation, focusing on the success it's had in rescuing and rehabilitating women and children caught up in a Nevada-based human trafficking ring. To that end, he lined up an interview with Devlin Saint—*the* Devlin Saint—for this afternoon.

It's not an investigative piece, but it's still important. Despite being relatively new, the Devlin Saint Foundation has become one of the world's foremost philanthropic organizations, with fingers in educational projects, criminal rehabilitation efforts, global development, anti-hunger, the arts, and so much more.

Its success, of course, is attributed to Saint himself, the mysterious, young, and extremely private founder of the organization. A man who started the DSF only five years ago and grew it into a world-renowned philanthropic enterprise. Whose reputation as a brilliant and generous global philanthropist is counterbalanced by his notoriety for being an arrogant and enigmatic loner whose business acumen and exceptional looks have paved the way to his foundation's success where his chilly personality could not.

I hesitated when Roger assigned the story, but ultimately agreed. After all, Saint is so enigmatic and well-known that the whole country will read the story, and that can only be good for my career.

Now, I wrap up the call with Roger, ostensibly because I need to get moving, but really because as soon as my mind turned to the foundation, it also turned to Alex. With a sigh, I take one more look at the town below.

From up here, it looks small and fragile. Like an architectural model. But I know the truth. Beneath its bright sunshine and sparkling waters, Laguna Cortez is nothing but death and loss, sharp edges and pain.

Despite having only two lanes and soft shoulders, Sunset Canyon Road is the main east-west thoroughfare for this Orange County town. With its gentle curves, it's also the easiest route down the hill.

But I don't need easy. Not now. Not even remotely.

So instead of meandering like someone's grandma down the main road, I hook the first left onto a tiny canyon road with no shoulders, serious drop-offs, and hairpin curves from hell.

I fly down the road, losing my cap in the process so that my hair whips around, stinging my cheeks. I ignore the discomfort. My attention is entirely on the road, on navigating this path. Right now, all I need is the wind in my face, the roar of Shelby's engine, and the euphoria of knowing that for this moment at least, I'm in total and complete control.

That's an illusion, of course, and no one knows it better than me. No one is ever in control of their destiny. Lives are lost. Dreams are shattered. Hearts are broken. Right now, I could hit a pothole and flip the car. I could die before I ever make it into Saint's office.

But that's the thrill, right? And when I finally pull into the foundation's parking lot, I'm back in control. Because once again, I've shown that bitch Fate my middle finger.

I've won.

For a moment, I simply sit in the driver's seat, relishing my victory. Then I adjust the rearview mirror, grab the brush I keep in the glove compartment and go to work on my loose, dark brown curls. I always drive with a cap, which tends to prevent the worst tangles, but since the thing went flying, right now, I'm a mess.

I end up opening the trunk and getting my toiletry bag out of my suitcase. It has a small bottle of Argan oil, and I use a few drops to ease the tangles free. After years of driving Shelby, I've learned what necessities to have on hand.

I take the opportunity to fix my makeup as well, using the rearview as a cosmetic mirror. Even having driven from LA with the top down, I'm still pretty put together, which is probably because I don't use that much makeup to start with. Some golden eyeshadow to highlight my brown eyes. A smidge of gloss. Mascara of course, and just a hint of blush.

Normally I'm not particular about my face and hair. Or my clothes for that matter. Sure, I enjoy dressing up for a night out, but my favorite part of being a reporter is living in jeans and a T-shirt. Because most days I'm sitting at my desk writing or working the phone.

Today, though, I want to look as professional as possible. I've never seen a photo of Saint where he doesn't look sharp. Hell, dead-to-rights perfect. And I'll be damned if I'll walk in there without looking like his equal. If nothing else, Roger expects that.

I stayed with friends in Los Angeles yesterday after taking five days to drive from New York so I'd have Shelby with me in California. This morning, I'd done lunch with my friends, then meandered my way down to Laguna Cortez. My plan is to bunk with Brandy while I write the article about the foundation and research the facts surrounding Uncle Peter. She moved back after college, and I called last night to tell her I'd meet up with her after my interview.

I dressed for the interview before leaving LA. A simple black pantsuit with a white silk tank and a loose-fitting blazer. I'm wearing flats at the moment, but I reach into the back and grab the killer Christian Louboutin pumps I'd stashed there earlier.

Designer shoes are my weakness, and since I can't actually afford them, I've made them a game, searching them out in consignment stores, thrift stores, and online sites like eBay. I found these a few months ago at an estate sale. A total score. They also have the advantage of adding much-needed inches to my usual five-foot-five frame, which is always nice in an inter-view. I can hold my own, but extra height gives extra confidence.

Once I'm all set, I grab my dad's battered leather satchel that I use as a briefcase, then slide out of the car. I pause for a moment to look at the impressive building rising from what was once the slab of a long-demolished grocery store, the concrete baked and cracked. It had been an eyesore of disputed owner-ship, and Alex and I would walk across it some nights when we'd head out together for ice cream.

We'd walk from Uncle Peter's house to Pacific Avenue, the east-west street that serves as the access point for the Arts District. We'd get our ice cream from the corner store, then walk south along the Pacific Coast Highway for about a mile before crossing the highway to this lot. Then we'd keep walking toward the ocean and our tidal pools.

"What a wreck," Alex said once, looking around at the cracked concrete and sunbaked weeds that marred the empty lot.

I'd looked around, then shrugged. "It's just concrete."

"It's an eyesore. Right here between the Coast Highway and the ocean. It deserves better."

"Well…" I cast about for a piece of discarded chalk. Kids used the lot to draw, so it wasn't hard to find. I bent down and wrote *El and Alex's place*, careful to use the nickname he'd started calling me a few weeks after our first kiss. Everyone else called me Ellie.

Then I'd grinned up at him. "It's ours now. We can imagine it's anything. Does that make it better?"

"Oh, El," he'd said, with that sweet, sexy smile. "It does. It really does."

Now, I stand frozen, lost in the memory. Then I swallow the lump in my throat and pull myself from the past. The building that now rises in front of me is all cement and steel and glass, with sleek lines and sharp angles. Five stories that sparkle in the sunlight, complemented by a wide swath of eco-friendly landscaping that peters out as it reaches the sandy beach.

It's absolutely stunning, but I don't like it at all.

Because this building isn't supposed to be here. And I don't care about the environmentally responsible xeriscaping or the locally sourced materials. I don't give a shit about the beauty of the angles or the way such a massive structure rises from the ground as if it is as native to the coastline as the craggy cliffs and rocky coves.

And I could care less about how the amazing Devlin Saint took a stretch of undeveloped land with disputed title, got it sorted out, and built something as remarkable as the DSF's offices.

Because this was our space. Our lot. And I hate Saint for stealing the memory from me.

A fresh burst of anger cuts through me. Not at Saint this time, or even Alex. No, this time, I'm angry at myself. Because Alex Leto was a prick. A manipulative son-of-a-bitch, and I don't owe him a thing, much less warm and fuzzy memories.

If I could banish him from my mind, I would, but at the very least, I need to exorcise the power he has over me. And, dammit, I'm going to start right now.

I draw in a series of deep breaths, purposefully gathering myself. Then I cup my hand over my forehead to shield my eyes from the sun as I reconsider the building. And this time I have to admit that it's not so bad. At least Saint got out there and built something. Took an eyesore and turned it into something stunning. All Alex Leto did was run.

I'd trusted him, and he'd ripped me to shreds.

But I'm smarter now. Stronger, too. Just like he said.

And you know what?

Fuck Alex Leto. Fuck him for leaving me during those already dark days. For slinking away without a word and never getting in touch again. For casting the final blow when I was already cracked and broken.

Mostly, fuck him for breaking my heart.

Want more?
Read The Fallen Saint Series
His touch is her sin. Her love is his salvation
My Fallen Saint
My Beautiful Sin
My Cruel Salvation

About the Author

J. Kenner (aka Julie Kenner) is the *New York Times*, *USA Today*, *Publishers Weekly*, *Wall Street Journal* and #1 International best-selling author of over one hundred novels, novellas and short stories in a variety of genres.

You can find her book/series list here!

Stay in touch with JK and be the first to know about new releases: **Just text: JKenner to 21000 to subscribe to JK's text alerts.**

J. Kenner Facebook Page
Facebook Fan Group
Newsletter

www.jkenner.com